The New Observer's Book of

WARSHIPS

Hugh W. Cowin

With 183 photographs
of 152 classes or types

Frederick Warne

FREDERICK WARNE
Penguin Books Ltd, Harmondsworth, Middlesex, England
Viking Penguin Inc., 40 West 23rd Street, New York, New York 10010, U.S.A.
Penguin Books Australia Ltd, Ringwood, Victoria, Australia
Penguin Books Canada Limited 2801 John Street, Markham, Ontario, Canada L3R 1B4
Penguin Books (N.Z.) Ltd, 182–190 Wairau Road, Auckland 10, New Zealand

First published 1983
Reprinted 1983
New edition 1986

ISBN 0 7232 1694 0

Printed and bound in Great Britain by
Butler & Tanner Ltd
Frome and London

CONTENTS

INTRODUCTION

When the first edition of this book was published in May 1983, the Falklands' conflict was very recent history; being just a year past. As the first major naval action for almost 37 years, the outcome and the lessons to be learnt from that campaign were of extreme interest to naval communities worldwide, even if many of the events and their ramifications were clearly predictable well in advance of that brief, but bloody, contest of arms.

While there are some senior voices who would attempt to disparage the impact of the Falklands' conflict on the ongoing development of warships and the way in which they will be operated, such arguments carry more than a tone of complacency. Indeed, viewed objectively, those events in South Atlantic waters during the spring of 1982 reveal a number of sobering lessons and pose even more unanswered questions.

In one way, the nature of the conflict followed the now set pattern of rapidly developing into a warship versus aircraft type of combat. What became clear very rapidly is that the modern warship is far more fragile and, hence, vulnerable than its predecessors. Here, it is particularly pertinent to further reflect on the additional potential losses that would have occurred to British naval surface units had many of the recorded strikes not been made with weapons that failed to explode. Certainly, there is an incontestable mass of evidence to indicate that to survive, even against fairly modestly performed manned aircraft attack, the modern warship needs to be equipped with an effective anti-air sensor/weapons fit. Palpably, many of the British warships were not so equipped. In the context of countering the latterday sea-skimming missile threat, the warship faces an even more severe threat, particularly in terms of ensuring not only that the missile is destroyed, but further, that it is killed sufficiently far off as to prevent potentially disabling shipboard damage from chunks of missile debris. The air threat embraces factors that clearly affect the future anti-air sensor/weapons selection process within a large number of navies. Significantly, the Soviets have been fielding a number of supersonic anti-ship missiles for many years now, while France is known to be actively developing its own anti-ship missile capable of arriving at its target at more than twice the speed of their existing Exocet. Just how effective the current generation of smaller calibre shipboard close-in weapons systems would prove to be against such faster missiles appears extremely conjectural.

Turning to the broader aspects of warship development, it is interesting to note that while both Italy and Spain have now constructed their own versions of the compact aircraft-carrier concept, the Soviets and France remain committed to constructing new nuclear-powered conventionally large aircraft carriers. Whether the compact carrier will meet with more general naval acceptance, particularly in the light of the emergence of helicopter/jump jet mercantile conversions, remains open to question.

NOTES ON THE BOOK

The contents have been arranged sectionally in such a way as to group together vessels of the same generic type, such as Cruisers, Destroyers, Frigates, Corvettes, etc. Within each section, vessels are grouped in descending order of displacement.

Abbreviations

bhp	brake horsepower
CODAG	These terms refer to propulsive machinery arrangements
CODOG	with CO referring to COmbining power transmission sys-
COSAG	tems, D for Diesel, G for Gas turbine, S for Steam, with the fourth letter, either A or O, standing for And or Or
ft	feet
IFF	Interrogation, Friend or Foe
m	metres
mm	millimetres
shp	shaft horsepower
VTOL	vertical take-off and landing (aircraft)
3-D	three-dimensional

PHOTOGRAPHIC ACKNOWLEDGEMENTS

The author wishes to thank the following navies and organisations for their generous assistance in providing photographic support, without which the work would have remained stillborn. My thanks go to the navies of Australia, Brazil, Canada, Denmark, Finland, France, Federal Germany, Greece, Italy, Japan, the Netherlands, New Zealand, Portugal, South Africa, Spain, Sweden, United Kingdom and the United States. Similarly, invaluable aid was provided by Bath Iron Works, Bazan, Bremer Vulkan, Blohm und Voss, Brooke Marine, General Dynamics, Hall Russell, Intermarine, Lurssen, Newport News Shipbuilding, Rolls-Royce, SFCN, Todd Shipyards, Vickers Shipbuilding, Vosper Thornycroft and Yarrow Shipbuilders.

Typhoon class   Submarines

The Typhoon's vast girth is clearly visible in this astern view.

Role: Strategic power projection.   **Builder:** Severodvinsk, USSR.
User: Soviet Navy.   **Crew:** around 150.
Basic data: 24,000 tons estimated dived displacement; 600.4 ft
(183 m) overall length; 75.1 ft (22.9 m) maximum beam.
Propulsion: 2 nuclear reactors/steam turbines (estimated total
120,000 shp), 2 propellers.
Sensors: 1 surface search radar; multiple passive and active sonars;
inertial navigation and fire control systems; automated action information data processing system.
Armament: 20 SS-N-18 or SS-N-20 intercontinental submarine-
launched ballistic missiles; 6 heavyweight anti-submarine torpedo
tubes.
Top speed: 30 knots dived.   **Range:** Unlimited.
Programme: With the lead boat launched in 1980, 3 Typhoon class
submarines had been built by early 1985, with construction of a pos-
sible further 5 boats being completed by the early 1990s.
Notes: The world's biggest submarine, the Typhoon class represents
the Soviet's response to the US Navy's Trident/Ohio class submarine
programme. As with the US Navy's Trident/Ohio class submarine combination, the SS-N-18 or SS-N-20/Typhoon class submarine's capability is awesome, particularly in the Soviet case, where the Typhoon
class can strike almost all US targets without ever leaving home waters,
thanks to the up to 4,479 nautical mile (8,300 km) range of the 6 to
9 re-entry vehicle-headed SS-N-20 nuclear missile.

This view of USS Michigan *(SSBN727) emphasises its great length, only marginally shorter than that of the Ticonderoga class cruiser.*

Role: Strategic power projection.
Builder: General Dynamics, USA.
User: US Navy.
Basic data: 18,700 tons dived displacement; 560 ft (170.7 m) overall length; 42 ft (12.8 m) maximum beam.   **Crew:** 157.
Propulsion: 1 General Electric S8G pressurised water nuclear reactor/ 1 General Electric geared steam turbine (60,000 shp); 1 propeller.
Sensors: BQQ-6 bow-mounted and towed array sonar system; 1 surface search radar; 2 SINS shipboard inertial navigational systems; MK 98 missile fire control system; automated action information data processor.
Armament: 24 Trident submarine-launched intercontinental ballistic missiles; 4 heavyweight anti-submarine torpedo tubes.
Top speed: Over 20 knots dived.   **Range:** Unlimited.
Programme: A planned 15 class, of which 11 had been ordered by the end of 1983. The class, along with their completion dates or projected deliveries, comprise: USS *Ohio* (SSBN726), October 1981; USS *Michigan* (SSBN727), September 1982; USS *Florida* (SSBN728), June 1983; USS *Georgia* (SSBN729), February 1984; USS *Henry M. Jackson* (SSBN730), October 1984; USS *Alabama* (SSBN731), June 1985; USS *Alaska* (SSBN732), February 1986; SSBN733, October 1986 and SSBN734, early 1987.
Notes: Much longer than their Lafayette/Franklin class predecessors, the Ohio class boats carry not only half as many again missiles, but also employ a more refined and quieter running propulsive system, itself some four times more powerful than that of the Lafayettes.

Britain's projected Trident missile-carrying boat for the 1990s.

Role: Strategic power projection.   **Builder:** Vickers, UK.
User: Under development for the Royal Navy.
Basic data: 15,000 tons dived displacement; 492.1 ft (150 m) overall length; 42.0 ft (12.8 m) maximum beam.   **Crew:** 150.
Propulsion: 1 Rolls-Royce PWR 2 pressurised water-cooled nuclear reactor/1 GEC steam turbine; 1 propeller.
Sensors: 1 Type 1006 surface search radar; 1 Type 2054 suite of active, passive, intercept and towed array sonars and processing systems; 1 Ferranti dual-key fire control system; inertial navigational system.
Armament: 16 Trident D5 submarine-launched intercontinental ballistic missiles; 4 heavyweight anti-submarine torpedo tubes.
Top speed: Over 25 knots dived.   **Range:** Unlimited.
Programme: This planned 4 boat class is being developed to replace Britain's ageing Polaris-carrying Resolution class strategic submarine force during the early 1990s. The UK Ministry of Defence Procurement Executive formally requested Vickers Shipbuilding and Engineering at Barrow-in-Furness to respond to a non-competitive tender for lead of class development and construction in October 1984.
Notes: The basic design of the UK SSBN 05 boats owes much to the earlier US *Ohio* class, but will be somewhat shorter as a result of its need to house only 16 missile silos, rather than the Ohio boats' 24. Similarly, as is British practice, the position of the hydroplanes will be shifted from the boat's sail, or conning tower, forward to the bow section. As with the US design, the Royal Navy class will have four deck levels.

Le Redoutable class　　　　　　　　　**Submarines**

The ballistic missile equipped Le Redoutable (*S611*).

Role: Strategic power projection.
Builder: Cherbourg, France.
User: French Navy.
Basic data: 9,000 tons divided displacement; 419.95 ft (128 m) overall length; 34.8 ft (10.6 m) maximum beam.　　　　**Crew:** 135.
Propulsion: 1 nuclear reactor/2 geared steam turbines; 1 propeller.
Sensors: 1 DUUV23 and DUUX2 active and passive sonar systems. 1 sea and navigational radar; automated fire control systems.
Armament: 16 M20 thermo-nuclear ballistic missiles; 4 light-weight anti-submarine torpedo tubes (18 torpedoes).
Top speed: 20 knots dived.　　　　　　　　　　**Range:** Unlimited.
Programme: Ordered on an incremental basis, the first 2 of this 7 boat class were authorised in 1963. The class comprises: *Le Redoutable* (*S611*), *Le Terrible* (S612), *Le Foudroyant* (S610), *L'Indomptable* (S613) and *Le Tonnant* (S614) plus 2 improved vessels *L'Inflexible* (S615) and S617. All first five boats were laid down between 1964 and 1973 and respectively entered service in December 1971, January 1973, June 1974, December 1976 and May 1980. *L'Inflexible* entered service in May 1985, to be followed by S615 in 1994.
Notes: Unlike the Royal Navy's Resolution class ballistic missile carrying submarines, which lean heavily on both US nuclear reactor and hull design, the Le Redoutable class boats are the result of the French Government's 1960 decision to develop their own nuclear-powered submarine and parallel ballistic missile programmes. As with other nuclear-powered submarines, this class of boat employs a hybrid propulsion system, using the nuclear reactor as its main power source, but backed by a diesel-electric auxiliary system, capable of a range of 5,000 nautical miles.

HMS Resolution (*S22*), *July 1982*.

Role: Strategic power projection   **Builders:** Various, UK.
User: Royal Navy.
Basic data: 8,400 tons dived displacement; 425 ft (129.5 m) overall length; 33 ft (10.1 m) maximum beam.   **Crew:** 143.
Propulsion: 1 Rolls Royce pressurised water nuclear reactor, 1 English Electric geared steam turbine (c. 20,000 shp); 1 propeller.
Sensors: 1 Type 1003 surface search radar; 1 type 2001 and 1 Type 2007 bow-mounted sonars; automated fire control system.
Armament: 16 Polaris A3 thermo-nuclear ballistic missiles; 6 tubes for heavyweight anti-submarine torpedoes.
Top speed: 25 knots dived.   **Range:** Unlimited.
Programme: The first of this 4 boat class was laid down at Vickers' Barrow-in-Furness yards in February 1964 and the last completed in late 1969. The class comprise; HMS *Resolution* (S22), HMS *Repulse* (S23), HMS *Renown* (S26) and HMS *Revenge* (S27), the first pair being built by Vickers and the second two being constructed by Cammell Laird of Birkenhead. The respective commissioning dates for the boats were October 1967, September 1968, November 1968 and December 1969.
Notes: Although differing considerably in detail , the overall design of the Resolution class is based on that of the US Navy's Lafayette class submarine, both in terms of their nuclear reactor and hull technology; the major external difference being that the Resolution class are fitted with bow section hydroplanes.

HMS Trafalgar *(S113) on sea trials, April 1983.*

Role: Anti-submarine.   **Builder:** Vickers, UK.
User: Royal Navy.
Basic data: 5,050 tons dived displacement; 280.2 ft (85.4 m) overall length; 32.25 ft (9.83 m) maximum beam.   **Crew:** 111.
Propulsion: 1 Rolls-Royce nuclear pressurised water reactor/1 steam turbine (20,000 shp) or 1 standby diesel-electric generator/electric motor; 1 propeller.
Sensors: 1 sea search and navigational radar; advanced passive and active sonar systems; automated action information and fire control data processing system.
Armament: 5 heavyweight anti-submarine torpedo tubes for launching either Mk 24 Tigerfish torpedoes or Sub-Harpoon anti-ship missiles.
Top speed: Over 30 knots dived.   **Range:** Unlimited.
Programme: A total 7 boat class, all of which had been ordered on an incremental basis by January 1986. Initially ordered in September 1977, the lead boat HMS *Trafalgar* (S113) was followed by HMS *Turbulent* (S114), HMS *Tireless* (S115), HMS *Torbay* (S116), HMS *Trenchant* (S91), HMS *Talent* (S92) and HMS *Triumph* (S93). The lead boat, *Trafalgar*, was laid down in April 1979, launched in July 1981, commissioned in late May 1983 and the first six boats are expected to be in service by the end of 1988.
Notes: The Trafalgar class design is an improved and slightly stretched derivative of the Swiftsure class. The Trafalgar class also incorporates an improved weapons fire control system. The crew complement of 111 is likely to be increased to around 115 as the class enters operational service.

Valiant class   Submarines

HMS Warspite *(S103), second of this Royal Navy five boat class.*

Role: Anti-submarine.   **Builders:** Various, UK.
User: Royal Navy.
Basic data: 4,900 tons dived displacement; 285.0 ft (86.9 m) overall
length; 33.2 ft (10.1 m) maximum beam.   **Crew:** 108.
Propulsion: 1 Rolls-Royce nuclear pressurised water reactor/1 geared
steam turbine (15,000 shp); 1 propeller.
Sensors: 1 Type 1003 sea search and navigational radar; 1 each of
Type 2001 active/passive and Type 2007 passive sonars; inertial
navigation and position fixing system; automated action information
data processing system.
Armament: 6 heavyweight anti-submarine torpedo tubes with 26 torpedoes or Sub-Harpoon submarine-launched anti-ship missiles.
Top speed: Around 30 knots.   **Range:** Unlimited.
Programme: This 5 boat class comprises: HMS *Valiant* (S102), HMS
Warspite (S103), HMS *Churchill* (S46), HMS *Conqueror* (S48) and
HMS *Courageous* (S50). *Valiant*, laid down at Vickers' Barrow shipyards in January 1962, was commissioned in mid-July 1966; the remaining four entering service in April 1967, July 1970, October 1971
and November 1971, respectively. All but the Cammell Laird built *Conqueror* were constructed by Vickers at Barrow-in-Furness.
Notes: The boats vary in detail between the first two and latter three
vessels, resulting in some Royal Navy submariners referring to the three
later boats as C class submarines. HMS *Valiant*, *Conqueror* and *Courageous* all participated in the Falklands campaign, with HMS *Conqueror*
being responsible for the sinking of the Argentinian cruiser *General
Belgrano*.

Tango class Submarines

A Soviet Navy diesel powered Tango class photographed in 1985.

Role: Anti-submarine.   **Builder:** Gorki, USSR.
User: Soviet Navy.
Basic data: 3,700 tons dived displacement; 300.2 ft (91.5 m) overall length; 29.5 ft (9.0 m) maximum beam.   **Crew:** 72.
Propulsion: 3 diesels/batteries/3 electric motors (6,000 shp), 3 propellers.
Sensors: 1 surface search radar; unidentified passive and active sonar systems; echo sounder; automated launch control system.
Armament: 6 forward-firing and 4 aft-firing heavyweight anti-submarine torpedo tubes for conventional or nuclear warhead-tipped torpedoes and SS-N-15 submarine-launched anti-ship missiles.
Top speed: 16 knots dived; 20 knots running on surface.
Range: 4,000 nautical miles dived at 8 knots with periodic snorkel.
Programme: Reported to have entered service with the Soviet Fleet during 1972, 18 of this class were believed to be operational by the end of 1984.
Notes: According to US naval technical intelligence assessments, the Tango class reflects some of the most modern diesel-electric submarine technology available, including having the hull coated in a sonar-absorbing rubber compound. While not as deep-diving as their stronger-hulled nuclear-powered contemporaries, the Tango class submarines, with their long endurance, make admirable boats for operation in such as the Mediterranean and Baltic.

One of the first views of the lead Kilo class submarines reveals the boat to have a relatively short hull, topped by an elongated and rectangular conning tower or 'sail'.

Role: Patrol.   **Builder:** (lead yard): Komsomolsk, USSR.
User: Soviet Navy.
Basic data: Estimated 3,200 tons dived displacement; 219.8 ft (67.0 m) overall length; 29.5 ft (9.0 m) maximum beam.
Crew: around 90.
Propulsion: Diesel-electric drive; no further data.
Sensors: Undesignated passive and active sonar systems.
Armament: Includes both nuclear warheaded and conventional 533 mm heavyweight anti-submarine torpedoes.
Top speed: Around 20 knots dived.   **Range:** No available data.
Programme: Believed to be a replacement for the ageing Foxtrot class diesel-electric submarines, the Kilo class will probably be built in fairly large numbers during the 1980s.
Notes: Built to fulfil the same requirements as set down for the Royal Navy's Vickers Type 2400 diesel-electric design, the emergence of the Kilo class was first noted in 1981, the first photographic evidence being published in the West towards the close of 1982. Of interest is the generally close similar external appearance of the Kilo class hull design to that of the earlier Dutch-developed Zwaardis class submarine. While clearly not as capable as the deep-diving, dedicated hunter/killer Alfa class submarines employed by the Soviets, the Kilo class programme is likely to cost considerably less, or, alternatively, provide many more Kilos than Alfas for the same outlay.

Rubis (*S601*), *lead boat of this French Navy class, 1981*.

Role: Anti-submarine.   **Builder:** DCAN, Cherbourg, France.
User: French Navy.
Basic data: 2,670 tons dived displacement, 236.2 ft (72 m) overall
length; 24.9 ft (7.6 m) maximum beam.   **Crew:** 66.
Propulsion: 1 pressurised water nuclear reactor; 1 electric motor; 1
propeller.
Sensors: 1 DRUA 33 surface search radar; passive and active sonar
and underwater telephone systems including 1 DSUV 22, 1 DUUA 2B
and 1 DUUX 2 equipment; echo sounder.
Armament: 4 forward-firing heavyweight anti-submarine torpedo
tubes for 14 torpedoes or SM 39 Exocet submarine-launched anti-ship
missiles or 533 mm (21 inch) mines.
Top speed: Over 25 knots dived.   **Range:** Unlimited.
Programme: This planned 8-boat class comprises; *Rubis* (S601),
Saphir (S602) *Casabianca* (S603) and S604 to S608. The lead
boat, *Rubis*, was laid down in December 1976, launched in July 1979
and entered service in July 1982, followed by *Saphir* in July 1984.
Programme schedules call for the delivery of the 3rd through 5th
boats between 1987 and 1990.
Notes: Powered by a 48-megawatt pressurised water reactor, driving
two turbo-alternators, the Rubis class hunter/killer submarines represent the French equivalent of the US Navy's Los Angeles class and the
Royal Navy's Trafalgar and Swiftsure class boats.

Upholder (Type 2400) class   Submarines

An artist's cutaway impression of the Upholder class boat.

Role: Patrol.   **Builder:** Vickers (lead yard), UK.
User: On order for the Royal Navy.
Basic data: 2,400 tons dived displacement; 230.5 ft (70.25 m) overall
length; 24.9 ft (7.6 m) maximum beam.   **Crew:** 46.
Propulsion: 2 Paxman Ventura diesel generators (total 2.015 bhp)/
batteries/1 GEC electric motor (5,400 shp); 1 propeller.
Sensors: 1 Kelvin Hughes Type 1006 surface search and navigational
radar; 1 Thomson-CSF Type 2040 passive sonar; Thomson-CSF Type
2019 passive/active sonar; Type 2026 towed array sonar; Omega very
low frequency underway navigational system; automated action information data processing and launch control system; 1 echo sounder.
Armament: 6 forward-firing heavyweight torpedo tubes for 18 tor-
pedoes/mines or Sub-Harpoon anti-ship missiles.
Top speed: 20 knots dived.
Endurance: Over 28 days on station, after a dived transit of 2,500
nautical miles and the same on return.
Programme: With preliminary design work completed during the late
1970s and referred to in the UK Defence Estimates paper of April 1980,
the lead of class contract was awarded to Vickers at the beginning of
November 1983 and could well run to an ultimate 14 boats. The lead
of class, HMS *Upholder* (S40), should be delivered during the late
1987/early 1988 period. The second, third and fourth boats in this
class were ordered from Cammell Laird in January 1986.
Notes: Designed as a replacement for the Royal Navy's Oberon class
submarines. Of conventional two-decked, single pressure hull design,
the Type 2400 can dive to depths in excess of 656 ft (200 m).

Type 206 class   Submarines

U13 of the Federal German Navy.

Role: Patrol.
Builders: Various, Federal German; Vickers, UK.
Users: Navies of Federal Germany (18) and Israel (3).
Basic data: 825 tons full displacement dived, 160.8 ft (49.0) overall length; 15.75 ft (4.8 m) maximum beam.   **Crew:** 22.
Propulsion: 2 MTU 820Db diesels (total 1,200 bhp)/batteries/1 electric motor (2,300 shp); 1 propellor.
Sensors: 1 sea search and navigational radar, 1 long range passive and 1 trainable active/passive sonars; 1 echo sounder.
Armament: 8 heavyweight anti-submarine torpedo tubes (16 torpedoes).
Top speed: 17 knots dived.   **Endurance:** Over 19 days at 12 knots.
Programme: A total of 21 Type 206 boats have been constructed comprising 18 for Federal Germany (*U13* through *U30*) and 3 for Israel (*Gal, Tanin* and *Rahav*). Howaldtswerke built the lead of class, plus 7 subsequent boats, while Nordseewerke constructed the other 10 vessels, all of which were delivered between April 1973 and March 1975. The 3 Vickers-built boats for Israel were delivered between December 1976 and December 1977.
Notes: A somewhat larger development of the earlier Type 205 boats. The submerged range of the Type 206 is reported to be 200 nautical miles (371 km) at a speed of 5 knots without recourse to snorkelling.

Nimitz class   Aircraft carriers

USS Nimitz *(CVN68) escorted by a California class cruiser.*

Role: Air power projection.   **Builder:** Newport News, USA.
User: US Navy.
Basic data: 93,405 tons full displacement; 1,092 ft (332.8 m) overall
length; 252 ft (76.8 m) maximum beam.   **Crew:** 6,280.
Propulsion: 2 Westinghouse A4W pressurised water nuclear reactors
powering steam turbines (total 280,000 shp); 4 propellers.
Sensors: Comprehensive suite of SPS-10 (surface) and SPS-43A or
SPS-48 (air) long-range radars; 3 Mk 115 fire control radars (Mk 91
systems substituted in CVN 70 onwards), all integrated and managed
by highly automated tactical action control systemry. 1 URN-20 or
-25 TACAN aircraft homer.
Armament: 1 air group of around 95 aircraft; 3 octuple Sea Sparrow
point defence surface-to-air missile launchers; 3 Phalanx 20 mm
rapid-fire gun close-in weapons systems (a 4th Phalanx is fitted to
CVN 70 onwards).
Top speed: 32 knots.   **Range:** Unlimited.
Programme: Originally conceived during the mid-1960s as a 3-ship
class to replace the Midway carriers, the contract for the lead ship,
USS *Nimitz* (CVN68), was placed in 1967, the next two ships, USS
Dwight D Eisenhower (CVN69) and USS *Carl Vinson* (CVN70), being
ordered in 1970 and 1974, respectively. *Nimitz* entered service in May
1975, followed by CVN69 in late 1977 and CVN70 in 1982. An order
for a fourth Nimitz class ship, USS *Theodore Roosevelt* (CVN71), was
placed in late 1980, with delivery planned for 1986. Two more carriers,
Abraham Lincoln (CVN72) for 1989 delivery and *George Washington*
(CVN73) for acceptance in 1991, were ordered in December 1982,
bringing the current class total to 6 carriers.
Notes: The largest aircraft carriers extant, the Nimitz class carriers
embody a 4.5 acre flightdeck layout based on that of the earlier,

conventionally-powered Kitty Hawk class, while the Nimitz class's nuclear reactor system is a much refined development of the 8 reactor installation used to power the USS *Enterprise* (CVN65), America's first nuclear-powered carrier. The nominal 13-year useful life of the Nimitz class's nuclear fuel rods provides the energy equivalent to 11 million barrels of fuel oil, giving the ships the ability to sail unrefuelled for between 800,000 and 1 million nautical miles. Of the total crew complement, 2,620, or just over 40 per cent, are aviation personnel. A typical air group embarked aboard these Nimitz class carriers comprise 2 squadrons of Grumman F-14 Tomcat all-weather fighters, 2 squadrons of Vought A-7 Corsair II attack types, 1 squadron of Grumman A-6E Intruder all-weather attack machines, 4 to 6 Grumman EA-6B Prowler electronic warfare types, 4 Grumman KA-6D Intruder tanker aircraft, along with 1 squadron of Lockheed S-3A Viking and 1 squadron of Sikorsky SH-3 Sea King helicopters for anti-submarine missions. For tactical airborne control and early warning, each of these carriers always operates with 4 Grumman E-2C Hawkeyes aboard.

USS Dwight D Eisenhower (*CVN69*) *accompanied by USS* California (*CGN36*).

Kitty Hawk class

Aircraft carriers

USS John F. Kennedy *(CV67) the improved last of class.*

Role: Air power projection.　　**Builders:** Various, USA.
User: US Navy.
Basic data: 80,800 tons full displacement; 1,062.5 ft (323.9 m) overall length; 250 ft (76.2 m) maximum beam.
Crew: 5,380, including 2,500 aviation personnel.
Propulsion: 4 Westinghouse geared steam turbines (total 280,000 shp); 4 propellers.
Sensors: 1 SPS-49 long-range air search radar, 1 SPS-48 height finder (3-D) radar; 1 SPS-10B surface search and navigational radar; 2 Mk 91 missile fire control systems; 1 URN-22 TACAN aircraft homer; 1 SQS-23 bow-mounted sonar (in CV66 only); 1 NTDS automated action information data processing system.
Armament: 1 air group of around 85 aircraft; 2 octuple Mk 29 launches for Sea Sparrow point air defence missiles in CV63, CV66 and CV67, while CV64 has twin Mk 10 launchers for Terrier area air defence missiles; 3 Phalanx 20 mm close-in weapons systems.
Top speed: 33 knots.　　**Range:** 8,000 nautical miles at 20 knots.
Programme: A 4 ship class comprising USS *Kitty Hawk* (CV63), USS *Constellation* (CV64), USS *America* (CV66) and USS *John F. Kennedy* (CV67); commissioned in April 1961, October 1961, January 1965 and September 1968, respectively.
Notes: Developed from the Forrestal class. *John F. Kennedy* incorporates certain improvements, including a fourth aircraft elevator and has an increased full displacement of 82,560 tons. While carrying fewer aircraft than the Nimitz class, the composition of the Kitty Hawk's air group is similar to that of the larger carriers.

Forrestal class   Aircraft carriers

USS Forrestal (*CV59*) *at sea in December 1975.*

Role: Air power projection.   **Builders:** Various, USA.
User: US Navy.
Basic data: 78,000 tons full displacement; 1,039 ft (316.7 m) overall
length; 238 ft (72.5 m) maximum beam.   **Crew:** 5,390.
Propulsion: 4 Westinghouse geared steam turbines (total
280,000 shp); 4 propellers.
Sensors: 1 SP3-43A (SPS-49 to be retrofitted) long-range air search
radar; 1 SPS-48 height finder (3-D) radar, 1 SPS-58 low-level air
threat warning radar; 1 SPS-10 surface search and navigational radar;
2 Mk 91 fire control radar systems for Sea Sparrow; 1 URN-22
TACAN aircraft homer; NTDS automated action information data processor.
Armament: 1 air group of up to 85 aircraft. Ships have or are being
fitted with 2 octuple Mk 25 or 29 launchers for Sea Sparrow point
air defence missiles; 3 Phalanx 20 mm close-in weapons systems are
being fitted as they become available.
Top speed: 32 knots.   **Range:** 8,000 nautical miles at 20 knots.
Programme: This 4 ship class comprises: USS *Forrestal* (CV59),
USS *Saratoga* (CV60), USS *Ranger* (CV61) and USS *Independence*
(CV62). Commissioning dates: October 1955. April 1956, August
1957 and January 1959, respectively.
Notes: These were the first post-World War II US carriers and are in
the process of being modernised under the US Navy's Service Life
Extension Programme (SLEP), starting with *Saratoga*, aimed at ex-
tending their lives by some 15 years.

Kiev class   Aircraft carriers

The second of class Minsk *at speed.*

Role: Fleet air defence.   **Builder:** Nikolayev, USSR.
User: Soviet Navy.
Basic data: 43,000 tons full displacement; 900 ft (270 m) overall
length; 164 ft (50 m) maximum beam.   **Crew:** 1,700.
Propulsion: 4 geared steam turbines (total 140,000 shp); 4 propellers.
Sensors: 1 long-range air search radar; 2 separate height finder (3-D)
radars (one probably for ship-controlled interception); 2 surface search
and navigational radars; 2 fire control radars each for the SA-N-3
and SA-N-4 missile systems; 1 fire control radar for the SS-N-12 missile system; 2 fire control radars for the 76 mm guns; 4 fire control
radars for the 30 mm Gatling guns. 1 hull-mounted and 1 towed variable depth sonar.
Armament: Typically 12 Yakolev Yak-36 VTOL strike fighters and 24
Kamov Ka 25 helicopters; 4 twin SS-N-12 anti-ship cruise missile
launchers; 2 twin SA-N-3 area air defence missile launchers; 2 twin
SA-N-4 short range air defence missile launchers; 1 twin SUW-N-1
short-range anti-submarine missile launcher; 2 twin 76 mm dual-purpose guns; 8 single 30 mm Gatling anti-aircraft guns.
Top speed: 32 knots.   **Range:** 13,500 nautical miles at 18 knots.
Programme: The first of this 4 ship class, *Kiev*, was laid down in
September 1970 and accepted into service in May 1975; a second
ship, *Minsk*, followed on to the stocks in December 1972 and was
accepted in February 1978. The third ship, *Kharkov*, laid down in
October 1975, entered service early in 1982, while the fourth vessel,
Novorossiysk, joined the Soviet Fleet in the late spring of 1983.
Notes: The Kiev class ships are not only the largest Soviet warships
yet to enter service, but with their complement of vertical take-off and
landing (VTOL) Yakolev Yak-36 'Forger' strike fighters, these ships
provide the Soviet Navy with a quantum jump in seagoing air capa-

bility. Unlike the earlier Moskva class helicopter cruisers, the Kiev class must be seen as real aircraft carriers, particularly when viewed in the light of recent successful operational deployment of the smaller HMS *Invincible* in the South Atlantic. Considering the previous total lack of Soviet navy fixed winged, carrier-going aircraft operating experience, the apparently trouble-free deployment of the just supersonic Yakovlev Yak-36 is particularly notable, as is the exceptionally heavy and well-balanced sensors/weapons fit installed aboard these ships. Indeed, in terms of both offensive and defensive armament, the Kiev class ships not only have much more capability than all but the much larger US carriers, but the Kiev class actually carries more onboard weaponry than just about any US warship, including the Virginia class nuclear powered cruisers. Range of the Kiev's SS-N-12 anti-ship cruise missiles is quoted as being around 300 nautical miles, while the Kiev class carry no less than a 5-tier air defence capability built around the 'Forger', the 30 nautical mile ranged SA-N-3 and 8 nautical mile ranged SA-N-4 missiles, backed by 76 mm and rapid fire 30 mm gun systems; all radar directed.

A close-up aspect of Kiev *that highlights the angled flight deck and sensor/weapon fit.*

Richelieu   Aircraft carriers

A model of France's projected nuclear-powered carrier.

Role: Air power projection.   **Builder:** DCN Brest, France.
User: French Navy.
Basic data: 36,000 tons full displacement; 853.0 ft (260.0 m) overall
length; 200.1 ft (61.0 m) maximum beam.   **Crew:** 1,700.
Propulsion: 2 pressurised water nuclear reactors (total 120,000 shp
estimated); 2 propellers.
Sensors: 1 DRBJ11B long range air search 3-D radar; 1 DRBV27 air
search radar; 1 DRBV15 low level air and sea search radar; 1 Vampir
infra red optronic fire control system for air defence missiles; SENIT
6 automated action information data processing.
Armament: 1 air group of 40 aircraft; 2 octuple Crotale Navale point
air defence missile launchers; 3 sextuple Sadrale point air defence
missile launchers.   **Top speed:** 28 knots.   **Range:** Unlimited.
Programme: A larger development of the earlier nuclear-powered
PH-75 or Provence class studies of the latter 1970s, design work on
the definitive *Richelieu* (R.) was initiated during 1980. Authorisation
for full-scale development on the lead carrier was provided in the
French 1984/88 defence budget plan. Scheduled to be laid down
during 1986, *Richelieu* should enter service in 1995. An as yet unnamed second of class carrier is expected to be authorised in the 1988/
92 French defence budget plan.
Notes: Designed to replace the existing pair of Clemenceau class aircraft carriers, the projected Richelieu class are physically larger than
their forebears, particularly in terms of both flight deck length and area.
Besides the normal ship's complement of 1,150, a further 550 aviators
personnel are needed to operate and maintain the 40 unit air group,
consisting of Dassault Super Etendard fixed winged strike aircraft and
anti-submarine helicopters (most probably Aerospatiale's navalised
Super Puma).

Clemenceau class   Aircraft carriers

Clemenceau (*R98*) *of the French Navy, 1976*.

Role: Air power projection.   **Builders:** Various, France.
User: French Navy.
Basic data: 32,780 tons full displacement; 869.4 ft (265 m) overall
length; 168 ft (51.2 m) maximum beam.   **Crew:** 1,338.
Propulsion: 2 Parsons geared steam turbines (total 126,000 shp); 2
propellers.
Sensors: 1 DRBV 20C long range air search radar; 1 DRBV 23B air
search radar; DRBI 10 height finder (3-D) radars; 1 DRBV 50 low-
level air and sea search radar; 1 Decca sea search and navigational
radar; 3 DRBC 31 and 2 DRBC 32 fire control radars for the 100 mm
guns; 1 URN 6 TACAN aircraft homer; 1 SQS 505 hull-mounted sonar;
SENIT II automated action information data processing system.
Armament: 1 air group of around 40 aircraft; 8 single 100 mm Model
1953 dual-purpose-guns.
Top speed: 32 knots.   **Range:** 7,500 nautical miles at 18 knots.
Programme: This 2 ship class, made up of *Clemenceau* (R98) and
Foch (R99), were authorised under the 1953 and 1955 French defence
budgets and were accepted into service in November 1961 and July
1963, respectively. *Clemenceau* underwent a major refit between late
1977 and late 1978, while *Foch* underwent a similarly extensive refit
during 1980.
Notes: The normal air group embarked comprises 16 Super Etendards
(strike), 3 Etendard IVP (reconnaissance), 10 F-8 Crusaders (fighters),
7 Alizes (anti-submarine) and 2 or 3 Alouette helicopters.

Invincible class   Aircraft carriers

HMS Ark Royal *(RO7); note her heightened ski-jump.*

Role: Multi-purpose   **Builders:** Various, UK.
User: Royal Navy.
Basic data: 19,500 tons full displacement; 677.8 ft (206.6 m) overall length; 90.2 (27.5 m) maximum beam.   **Crew:** 903.
Propulsion: 4 Rolls-Royce TM3B Olympus turbines (total derated 79,200 shp); COGAG; 2 c-p propellers.
Sensors: 1 Type 1022 long-range air search radar; 1 Type 922-low-level air and sea search radar; 1 Type 1006 sea search and navigational radar; 2 Type 909 missile fire control radars; 1 Type 184 hull-mounted sonar; ADAWS 5 automated action information data processing.
Armament: 1 air group of, typically, 14 aircraft; 1 twin Mk 30 launcher for Sea Dart area air defence missiles, being equipped with 2 Phalanx 20 mm close-in weapons systems.
Top speed: 28 knots.   **Range:** 5,000 nautical miles at 18 knots.
Programme: This 3 ship class consists of HMS *Invincible* (R05), HMS *Illustrious* (RO6) and HMS *Ark Royal* (RO7). Ordered incrementally in April 1973, May 1976 and December 1978, the lead ship was constructed at Vickers' Barrow-in-Furness yards, while the 2nd and 3rd ships were built at Swan Hunter on the Tyne. *Invincible* was commissioned in March 1980, followed by *Illustrious* in June 1982 and *Ark Royal* in November 1985.
Notes: The history of these large, rather stark ships is one of extremely chequered fortunes right up until 1982 when the existence of the lead

ship, *Invincible*, alone made the mounting of a British task force to the Falklands feasible. Prior to that point, these rather modestly sized VTOL aircraft carriers had come in for a lot of criticism, particularly on grounds of cost (the 1st ship cost £175 million). Indeed, in March 1982, the UK Minister of Defence announced that *Invincible* was to be sold to the Royal Australian Navy in late 1983 as part of a general reduction in Royal Navy force levels. Within a space of less than two months *Invincible*, along with HMS *Hermes* (R12), was providing the initial vital air cover for the Falklands bound force, as well as supplying an equally essential contribution by providing a major share of the Sea King anti-submarine helicopter force. Unlike the highly specialised functional solutions provided by the Sheffield and Broadsword class ships, the Invincibles were always intended to fill a multiplicity of roles. These range from fleet air defence to providing anti-submarine helicopter support, as well as acting as task group command ship.

A helicopter pilot's eye view of HMS Illustrious (*R06*).

Principe de Asturias type   Aircraft carriers

The ship seen during its 22nd May 1982 launching.

Role: Tactical air and anti-submarine.   **Builder:** Bazan, Spain.
User: Royal Spanish Navy.
Basic data: 15,000 tons full displacement; 640.0 ft (195.1 m) overall length; 80.0 ft (24.4 m) maximum beam.   **Crew:** 774.
Propulsion: 2 General Electric LM2500 gas turbines (total derated to 40,000 shp); 1 controllable pitch propeller.
Sensors: 1 SPS-52C air search and height finder (3-D) radar; 1 SPS-55 surface search and navigational radar; 1 SPN-35A aircraft precision approach control radar; 1 URN-22 TACAN aircraft homing radar.
Armament: 3 Matadors (Harriers); 14 Sikorsky SH-3D Sea King helicopters; 2 lighter anti-submarine helicopters; 4 Meroka 20 mm close-in anti-air weapons systems; mines.
Top speed: 26 knots.   **Range:** 7,500 nautical miles at 20 knots.
Programme: The *Principe de Asturias* (R11) was ordered in June 1977, laid down in October 1979, launched in May 1982 and scheduled to enter service during 1985. A second vessel is planned.
Notes: Designed by the US naval architects Gibbs and Cox for the now cancelled US Navy's Sea Control Ship requirement, this ship is one of the new breed of compact, through deck VTOL aircraft carriers initiated by the Royal Navy's Invincible class. Lighter than the Invincibles, but heavier than Italy's Garibaldi design, the Spanish carrier has 2 aircraft elevators, one on the starboard side immediately forward of the ship's bridge, while the other, when elevated, forms a centreline extension to the aft end of the flight deck. Steel is the basic material employed throughout both hull and superstructure, in an effort to minimise the effects of combat damage. The ship's 4 Meroka 20 mm gun mounts are installed high on the superstructure, the forward pair being set side by side just forward and below the wheelhouse, while the aft guns are mounted in staggered tandem (one above the other) at the aft end of the 'island', as a carrier's superstructure is known.

Garibaldi type

Aircraft carriers

Garibaldi (*R551*) under tow and showing her forward flight deck ski-jump to advantage.

Role: Anti-submarine and amphibious assault.
Builder: Italcantieri, Italy.
User: Italian Navy.
Basic data: 13,370 tons full displacement; 591.2 ft (180.2 m) overall length; 99.7 ft (30.4 m) maximum beam.
Crew: 560.
Propulsion: 4 Fiat-built General Electric LM2500 gas turbines (total derated to 80,000 shp); COGAG; 2 controllable-pitch propellers.
Sensors: 1 Selenia RAN-3L long range air search and height finder (3-D) radar; 1 Selenia RAN-106 medium range air/sea search radar; 1 Selenia RAN-205 surface search and navigational radar; 2 Selenia/ SMA RTN-30X Albatros system fire control radars; 3 Selenia/SMA RTN-20X 40 mm close-in weapons fire control radars; 1 Raytheon DE 1160 bow-mounted sonar; 1 TACAN aircraft homing radar; Selenia IPN-10 automated action information data processing system.
Armament: 18 Augusta-Sikorsky SH-3D Sea King helicopters; 4 single OTO-Melara Otomat Mk 2 anti-ship missile launchers; 2 octuple Albatros point air defence missile launchers; 3 twin 40 mm Breda/ Bofors close-in anti-war weapons; 2 triple Mk 32 lightweight anti-submarine torpedo tubes.
Top speed: 29.5 knots. **Range:** Over 7,000 nautical miles at 20 knots.
Programme: Ordered in November 1980, the *Giuseppe Garibaldi* was laid down in March 1981 and entered service in October 1985.
Notes: The *Garibaldi*'s design, in mission terms, is much closer to the Soviet's Kiev class than that of either of its British or Spanish contemporaries; an aspect underscored by *Garibaldi*'s respectable anti-ship missile fit and 2-tier shipboard anti-air capability. The ship also has space to accommodate up to 265 marine commandos. Although the Italian Navy has no Harrier-type aircraft, it has been decided to equip the carrier with a forward ski-jump in order to meet NATO forces' inter-operability requirements.

Iowa class

USS Iowa (BB61) The three white bulb-like objects visible high amidships are Mk 15 Phalanx weapons.

Role: Power projection.

Builder: Navy Dockyards, USA.

User: US Navy.

Basic data: 57,500 tons full displacement; 887.6 ft (270.5 m) overall length; 108.2 ft (33 m) maximum beam.   **Crew:** around 1,620.

Propulsion: 4 geared steam turbines (total 212,000 shp); 4 propellers.

Sensors: 1 SPS-49 long-range air search radar; 1 SLQ-32 electronics warfare suite. NTDS automated action information processing system.

Armament: Facilities for up to 4 Sikorsky SH-60 Seahawk helicopters; 8 quadruple Tomahawk cruise missile launchers; 4 quadruple Harpoon anti-ship missile launchers; 3 triple 16 inch guns; 6 twin 5 in Mk 28 dual-purpose guns; 4 Phalanx 20 mm close-in weapons systems, as currently being installed.

Top speed: 33 knots.   **Range:** 16,000 nautical miles at 15 knots.

Programme: Planned as a 6 ship class, only 4 were completed; USS *Iowa* (BB61), USS *New Jersey* (BB62), USS *Missouri* (BB63) and USS *Wisconsin* (BB64); all 4 being commissioned between February 1943 and April 1944. All 4 ships are being refurbished with USS *New Jersey* recommissioning in January 1983. The next battleship, *Iowa* (BB61), recommissioned in April 1984, with the remaining two ships scheduled for recommissioning in early and late 1987, respectively.

Notes: Being rebuilt as true multi-purpose ships, the Iowa class, thanks to its Tomahawk missile fit, will, in terms of their operational strike capability, serve as something of a cross between the tactical aircraft carrier and the strategic missile-carrying submarine, while retaining their big guns for long range shore bombardment. These guns can deliver a 2 ton shell to a maximum range of around 20 nautical miles (37 km) against surface targets. Similarly, as these ships were designed to withstand hits from just such shells, they should be far less vulnerable to missile strikes. The current modernisation programme is only a partial portion of that initially envisaged by the US Navy. As foreseen in the mid-1970s, each ship would have had its aft-mounted 16-inch gun turret removed and aft section modified to house and operate more anti-submarine helicopters. While there has been some US Congressional resistance to such a move, the prospect of seeing this type of subsequent major refit cannot be discounted. The ships' triple-barrelled 16-inch gun turrets are manually loaded, each requiring a gun crew of no less than 87 men. Including the below deck armoured ammunition lift, each turret installation has a total weight of 1,700 tons without ammunition.

USS Iowa (BB61) releases a salvo from her forward 16-inch turret.

Kirov class   Cruisers

An extremely informative view of Frunze *showing her forward missile silo banks and aft 130 mm gun mount.*

Role: General-purpose.   **Builder:** Baltic Yard, Leningrad, USSR.
User: Soviet Navy.
Basic data: 23,400 tons full displacement; 810 ft (245 m) overall length; 91.9 ft (28 m) maximum beam.   **Crew:** Around 800.
Propulsion: 2 sets of nuclear reactors plus oil-fired superheat booster boilers, each powering a geared steam turbine and propeller shaft (estimated total 150,000 shp), 2 propellers.
Sensors: 1 long-range air search radar; 1 height finder (3-D) radar; 1 each fire control radar for SS-N-19, SA-N-6 and SS-N-14 missiles; 2 fire control radars for SA-N-4 missiles; 1 fire control radar for 100 mm guns; 2 fire control radars for 30 mm guns; 1 hull-mounted sonar; 1 towed variable depth sonar; automated action information data processing system and long range (satellite) data links.
Armament: 3 Kamov Ka-26 'Hormone' or Ka-27 'Helix' helicopters; 20 SS-N-19 anti-ship cruise missiles in individual launch silos; 12 SA-N-6 area air defence missiles in individual vertical-launch silos; 1 twin SS-N-14 anti-submarine missile launcher; 2 fore and 2 aft quadruple vertical launchers for SA-N-8 short range air defence missiles on *Frunze*; 2 twin SA-N-4 point air defence missile launchers; 2 single 100 mm dual-purpose guns on *Kirov*, replaced by 1 twin 130 mm

dual-purpose gun on *Frunze*; 8 single 30 mm Gatling-type anti-aircraft guns; 2 twelve-barrel 250 mm anti-submarine rocket launchers.

Top speed: Over 33 knots. **Range:** Unlimited.

Programme: *Kirov*, the lead ship of this as yet indeterminate-sized class, was reported to have been laid down in 1973, launched in 1977 and entered trials in September 1980. A 2nd ship of this class, *Frunze*, laid down in January 1978, was launched in June 1981 and entered service during 1984. US naval intelligence report that a 3rd ship was started in 1983 and anticipate the completion of a 4th of class prior to the end of the 1980s.

Notes: Certainly the largest and most powerful ship built to meet the conventional heavy cruiser role anywhere in the world since the end of World War II, the *Kirov*'s finely proportioned lines and weight indicate an extremely efficient hull design, married to a form of construction capable of withstanding far more combat damage than any of its Western world contemporaries. Turning to the operational requirement aspect, *Kirov*'s primary role appears precisely to parallel that of the US Navy's California/Virginia classes of cruiser, namely that of acting as the main defensive screen for a carrier-centred task force, particularly in the light of the noticeable shift towards a primary anti-air defence weapon/sensor fit adopted for *Frunze*. As with their US rivals, these ships carry the necessary mass of communications equipment to enable them to act as command ships for a non-carrier group. *Kirov*'s sensor/weapons fit is extremely impressive, being both heavy and well balanced to meet the demands of the modern naval need to fight a potentially fully 3-dimensional threat. The anti-ship SS-N-19 has an effective range out to around 300 nautical miles (556 km), whilst the SA-N-6 area air defence missiles are reported to be effective out to a range of 40 nautical miles (74 km) and up to an altitude of 100,000 feet (30,480 m).

Kirov. *Note how her superstructure literally bristles with sensors.*

Moskva *displaying her somewhat stark, angular appearance.*

Role: Anti-submarine.   **Builder:** Nikolayev, USSR.
User: Soviet Navy.
Basic data: 17,000 tons full displacement; 623 ft (190 m) overall length; 111.5 ft (34 m) maximum beam.   **Crew:** 850.
Propulsion: 2 geared steam turbines (total 100,000 shp); 2 propellers.
Sensors: 1 long-range air search radar; 1 height finder (3-D) radar; 3 sea search and navigational radars,; 2 fire control radars (missile); 2 fire control radars (57 mm guns); 1 hull-mounted sonar; 1 towed, variable depth sonar; IFF and aircraft homing aids; automated action information data processing system.
Armament: 18 Kamov Ka-25 helicopters; 2 twin SA-N-3 area air defence missile launchers; 1 twin SUW-N-1 short-range anti-submarine missile launcher; 2 twin 57 mm anti-aircraft guns; 2 RBU 6000 twelve-barrel 250 mm anti-submarine rocket launchers.
Top speed: 30 knots.   **Range:** 7,000 nautical miles at 15 knots.
Programme: This 2 ship class, the initial unit of which was laid down in 1962, comprises *Moskva* and *Leningrad*, which entered service with the Soviet fleet in 1967 and 1968, respectively.
Notes: Although not the first post-World War II hybrid ship (half cruiser, half helicopter carrier) to emerge (that honour must go to the French Navy's *Jeanne d'Arc*), the Moskva class display a typically aggressive Russian design approach to meeting a stated operational requirement.

One of the remaining standard Sverdlov class cruisers.

Role: General-purpose.   **Builders:** Various, USSR.
User: Soviet Navy.
Basic data: 17,200 tons full displacement; 689 ft (210 m) overall
length; 70.85 ft (21.6 m) maximum beam.   **Crew:** 1,010.
Propulsion: 2 geared steam turbines (total 100,000 shp); 2 propellers.
Sensors: 3 separate long range air search radars; 1 sea search and
navigational radar; 16 fire control radars consisting of 4 differing types.
Armament: 4 triple 152 mm guns; 6 twin 100 mm dual-purpose guns;
16 twin 37 mm anti-aircraft (5 of this class also carry 8 twin 30 mm
anti-aircraft guns in addition to 37 mm guns); mines. Note: 2 Modified
Sverdlovs carry 1 twin SA-N-4 point air defence missile launcher in
place of either one or both of the aft 152 mm turrets. Another Modified
Sverdlov carries 1 twin SA-N-2 area air defence missile launcher in
place of third, or 'X' turret.
Top speed: 32 knots.   **Range:** 8,400 nautical miles at 15 knots.
Programme: An original 14 ship class built in 3 separate shipyards
during the early 1950s, 9 standard and 3 Modified Sverdlovs to remain
in use.
Notes: Rather handsome, twin-funnelled cruisers of conventional
World War II-period appearance, 2 of the Sverdlovs were converted to
command cruisers, and 1 into a guided missile cruiser. All retain at
least six of the originally fitted largest calibre guns, whilst nine of the
class retain all twelve big guns for use in onshore bombardment.

The French Navy's Jeanne d'Arc (R97) entering port, 1980.

Role: Multi-purpose.　　　　　**Builder:** DCAN Brest, France.
User: French Navy.
Basic data: 12,365 tons full displacement; 597.1 ft (182.0 m) overall length; 78.7 ft (24.0 m) maximum beam.　　　　**Crew:** 627.
Propulsion: 2 Rateau-Bretagne geared steam turbine (total 40,000 bhp); 2 propellers.
Sensors: 1 DRBI 10 air search and height finder (3-D) radar; 1 DRBV 22D air search radar; 1 DRBV 50 combined low-level air and sea search radar; 1 DRBN 32 sea search and navigational radar; 3 DRBC 32A gunfire control radars; 1 TACAN aircraft homer; 1 SQS 503–2 hull-mounted sonar system; SENIT II automated action information data processing system.
Armament: Up to 8 Aerospatiale Puma helicopters; 6 MM38 Exocet anti-ship missile launchers; 4 single 100 mm Model 1953 dual-purpose guns.
Top speed: 28 knots.　　　**Range:** 6,800 nautical miles at 16 knots.
Programme: Authorised in 1957. *Jeanne d'Arc* (R97) was laid down in July 1960, launched in September 1961 and entered service at the end of June 1964. The ship is scheduled to remain in service until the year 2004.
Notes: *Jeanne d'Arc* was the first of the post-World II generation of hybrid cruiser/helicopter carriers. *Jeanne d'Arc* is primarily employed in peacetime as a training ship, but in operational terms can be readily used as an anti-submarine helicopter platform, a helicopter-equipped amphibious assault ship, or a fairly major troop and equipment transport asset.

Colbert type   Cruisers

Colbert (*C611*) *seen prior to the fitting of Exocet.*

Role: Anti-aircraft.   **Builder:** DCAN Brest, France.
User: French Navy.
Basic data: 11,300 tons full displacement; 590.5 ft (190 m) overall length; 66.25 ft (20.2 m) maximum beam.   **Crew:** 562.
Propulsion: CEM Parsons geared steam turbines (total 86,000 shp); 2 propellers.
Sensors: 1 DRBV 51 and 1 DRBV 23C air search radars; 1 DRBI 10D height finder (3-D) radar; DRBV 50 surface search and navigational radar; 2 DRBR 51 Masurca fire control radars; 2 DRBC 31 fire control radars (57 mm guns); 1 DRBC 32C 100 mm gun fire control radar; 1 TACAN aircraft homer; SENIT automated action information data processor.
Armament: 4 Exocet anti-ship missile launchers; 1 twin Masurca area air defence missile launcher (48 missiles); 2 single 100 mm dual-purpose guns; 6 twin 57 mm anti-aircraft guns.
Top speed: 32 knots.   **Range:** 4,000 nautical miles at 25 knots.
Programme: Originally ordered in 1953, the sole *Colbert* (C611) was laid down in December 1953, launched in March 1956 and joined the fleet in May 1959.
Notes: *Colbert* initially mounted no less than sixteen 127 mm dual-purpose guns that have now been replaced by the 30 nautical mile ranged, near Mach 3 Masurca missiles and the 2 forward 100 mm guns. During the ship's most recent refit, racking to carry 4 Exocet container/launchers has been added, two each flanking the structure just forward of the bridge.

Slava, *the lead ship of this new Soviet cruiser class, whose primary armament is the around 300-nautical-mile (556 km) ranging SS-N-12 anti-ship cruise missile.*

Role: Anti-ship.   **Builder:** Nikolayev (lead), USSR.
User: Soviet Navy.
Basic data: 11,250 tons full displacement; 603.7 ft (184.0 m) overall length; 63.2 ft (19.25 m) maximum beam.   **Crew:** 650.
Propulsion: 4 gas turbines (total 120,000 shp); 2 propellers.
Sensors: 1 each of 2 separate types of long-range air search and height finder (3-D) radars; 1 IFF radar; 3 sea search and navigational radars; 4 separate types of fire control radar and optronic fire control radar/director systems for the ship's missiles and guns; 2 TACAN type aircraft homers; bow-mounted and variable depth sonar systems; automated action information data processing and satellite-fed data link systems.
Armament: 1 Kamov Ka-32 'Helix' helicopter; 8 twin SS-N-12 anti-ship cruise missile launchers; 1 octuple SA-N-6 vertically launched area air defence missile silo; 2 twin SA-N-4 point air defence missile launchers; 1 twin 130 mm dual-purpose gun; 6 multi-barrelled 30 mm Gatling type close-in weapons systems; 2 twelve-barrelled 250 mm RBU-6000 anti-submarine rocket launchers; 10 heavyweight anti-submarine torpedo tubes.
Top speed: 31 knots.   **Range:** 10,000 nautical miles at 15 knots.
Programme: *Slava*, the lead of class ship was reported to have been laid down in 1976, launched in 1979 and entered service in late 1982, with the Soviet's Black Sea Fleet. Two more of this class were said to have been laid down in 1978 and 1979, reportedly to enter service in

1983 and 1984, respectively. Just how many of these cruisers will be built remains a matter of some conjecture, but could total up to 8 ships.

Notes: The Slava class is seen as something of an enigma in Western naval intelligence circles, who view the design as being a curious mixture of something old, something new and certainly much borrowed from the preceding Kara class cruisers. Previously referred to as the BLK-COM-1, or Black Sea Combatant-1 class, these ships were clearly designed as dedicated anti-ship counters to surface elements of the US Navy's Mediterranean-based 6th Fleet; a conclusion borne out by the not inconsiderable, but essentially defensive anti-submarine sensor/weapons fit installed. The hull design of the Slava class appears to be a simply scaled-up duplicate of that of the Kara class vessel, with the Slava class probably employing a common-to-Kara propulsion machinery package. Unlike the Kara class, however, the Slava design has a taller, much more conventional looking superstructure that appears far less bedecked with radar aerials than its forebear.

Slava, *shown here wearing her more recent pennant number 108.*

USS Arkansas (*CGN41*), *in late 1980.*

Role: General purpose.   **Builder:** Newport News, USA.
User: US Navy.
Basic data: 11,000 tons full displacement; 585 ft (178.3 m) overall length; 63 ft (19.2 m) maximum beam.   **Crew:** 519.
Propulsion: 2 pressurised water D2G nuclear reactors/steam turbines (total 60,000 shp); 2 propellers.
Sensors: 1 SPS-40B long-range air search radar; 1 SPS-48C height finder (3-D) radar; 1 SPS-55 sea search and navigational radar; 2 SPG-51D and 1 SPG-60 fire control radars (missiles); 1 SPQ-91A fire control radar (guns and ASROC); 1 SQS-53 bow-mounted sonar; NTDS automated action information data processing system.
Armament: 1 Kaman SH-2 Seasprite helicopter; 2 twin Mk 26 launchers for Standard area air defence missiles (the forward Mk 26 launcher also handles ASROC anti-submarine missiles); 2 single 5 inch Mk 45 dual-purpose guns; 2 triple lightweight anti-submarine torpedo tubes. (Tomahawk cruise missiles and Harpoon anti-ship missiles are scheduled to be fitted to these cruisers during the early 1980s, as will be 2 Phalanx 20 mm close-in weapons systems.)
Top speed: 30 knots.   **Range:** Unlimited.
Programme: Like the preceding California class cruisers, the 4 ship Virginia class programme started life with much larger envisaged numbers than were actually achieved; the real constraint proving to be the eco-politically induced reduced fleet strength plans that emerged during the latter half of the 1970s. All 4 ships, USS *Virginia* (CGN38), USS *Texas* (CGN39), USS *Mississippi* (CGN40) and USS *Arkansas* (CGN41), were laid down between August 1972 and January 1977 and their respective commissioning dates were: September 1976, September 1977, August 1978 and October 1980.
Notes: Designed to act as large, high capability escorts for nuclear-

powered carriers, the Virginia class ships are larger, improved versions of the California class nuclear-powered cruisers. Although not immediately apparent, one of the Virginia class's major advances is the incorporation of a helicopter hangar under the stern flight pad, similar to that employed in the earlier Italian cruiser, *Vittorio Veneto*. While acting as a carrier escort, the Virginia class's primary role is to provide area air defence, and to this end the ships are equipped with Standard missiles which have a 30 nautical mile, or 56 km range (improvements to the Standard should extend its effective range out to 65 nautical miles, or 121 km). Having said this, it is interesting to compare the anti-air weaponry of these US ships with that to be found aboard the Soviet's smaller Kara and Kresta classes of cruiser.

USS Texas *(CGN39) showing her primary weapons disposition to advantage.*

Kara class   Cruisers

Tallin, *the last of class with her weapons clearly visible from this angle.*

Role: Anti-submarine.   **Builder:** Nikolayev, USSR.
User: Soviet Navy.
Basic data: 9,700 tons full displacement; 574 ft (175.0 m) overall length; 60 ft (18.3 m) maximum beam.   **Crew:** 520.
Propulsion: 4 gas turbines (total 120,000 shp); 2 propellers.
Sensors: 1 long-range air search radar; 1 height finder (3-D) radar; 2 surface search and navigational radars; 2 surface-to-air missile fire control radars; 2 each fire control radars for 76 mm and 30 mm gun systems; 1 hull-mounted sonar; 1 towed variable depth sonar.
Armament: 1 Kamov Ka-26 'Hormone' helicopter; 2 quadruple SS-N-14 anti-submarine missile launchers; 2 twin SA-N-3 surface-to-air missile launchers; 2 twin SA-N-4 surface-to-air missile launchers; 2 twin 76 mm dual-purpose guns; 4 single 30 mm Gatling anti-aircraft guns; 2 twelve-barrel RBU-6000 anti-submarine rocket launchers; 2 five-tube heavyweight anti-submarine launchers.
Top speed: 32 knots.   **Range:** 8,000 nautical miles at 15 knots.
Programme: The first of this 7 ship class was laid down during 1969 and joined the Soviet fleet in 1973. Delivery of this ship, *Nikolayev*, was followed by *Ochakov* (1974), *Kerch* (1975), *Azov* (1976), *Petropavlovsk* (1977), *Taskent* (1978) and *Tallin* (1979). The fourth ship. *Azov*, has undergone extensive modification to its aft sections, reportedly to act as trials ship for a new, vertically-stowed surface-to-air

missile system being developed for the new classes of Soviet cruisers and heavy destroyers now under construction.

Notes: The Kara class represents a larger and heavier follow-on to the Soviet first-generation Kresta II anti-submarine cruisers and carries the same primary armament of 8 SS-N-14 'Silex' 25 nautical mile (46 km) ranged missiles. Where the Karas differ from their forebears is in the adoption of gas turbine propulsion (the first application to a Soviet cruiser) and the incorporation of a SA-N-4 short-range (out to around 8 nautical miles/15 km) surface-to-air missile system to back up the ships' primary defensive armament of out to 30 nautical mile (55.5 km) SA-N-3 missiles. Any aircraft or missile penetrating these two outer defensive zones would still have to contend with the ships' not inconsiderable gun armament combination of out to around 5 nautical mile (8.25 km) ranging 76 mm fire and the very high rate 30 mm Gatling gun close-in weapons systems, reported to be highly effective out to around 2 nautical miles (3.7 km). Although marginally lighter and smaller than the contemporary US Navy California class nuclear-powered cruisers, the Kara class's heavy armament provides an interesting comparison between the two generally similar sized ships, particularly in terms of the broader spectrum of weapons fitted to the Soviet cruisers.

A Kara class cruiser of the Soviet Navy's Black Sea Fleet.

Ticonderoga class

USS Valley Forge (*CG50*) *showing to advantage the blend of Spruance class hull lines and Kidd class forward gun and missile launcher armament.*

Role: Area air defence.
Builders: Ingalls Shipbuilding and Bath Iron Works, USA.
User: US Navy.
Basic data: 9,600 tons full displacement; 567.0 ft (172.8 m) overall length; 55 ft (16.8 m) maximum beam. **Crew:** 360.
Propulsion: 4 General Electric LM2500 gas turbines (total 80,000 shp); COGAG; 2 controllable-pitch propellers.
Sensors: 1 SPS-49 long range air search radar; 1 SPS-55 surface search radar; 1 SPY-1A multi-function radar; 1 SQS-53A bow-mounted sonar; Mk 1 command and decision action data processing system.
Armament: 2 Sikorsky SH-60B Seahawk helicopters; 2 twin Mk 26 (early ships) or 2 Ex Mk 41 vertical missile launchers compatible with Standard MR or ER area air defence missiles on CG52 and onwards; Harpoon anti-ship missiles or ASROC anti-submarine missiles; 2 single 5-inch Mk 45 dual-purpose guns; 2 Mk 15 Phalanx 20 mm close-in weapons systems; 2 triple lightweight anti-submarine torpedo tubes.
Top speed: 32 knots. **Range:** 6,000 nautical miles at 20 knots.
Programme: Studied in conceptual form since the late 1960s under the US Navy's Aegis sea-going air defence requirement, early studies centred on a derivative of the Virginia class nuclear-powered cruiser, but this was ultimately dropped in favour of the CG 47, or Ticonderoga class ship, itself a development of the existing Spruance and Kidd class destroyers. The first of this currently 19 ship class, USS *Ticon-*

deroga (CG47) was initially contracted in September 1978 and commissioned in January 1983. USS *Yorktown* (CG 48) and USS *Vincennes* (CG 49) entered service in mid 1984 and 1985, respectively. By January 1986, a total of 19 of this class had been authorised, with USS *Vincennes* (CG 49), *Valley Forge* (CG 50), *Bunker Hill* (CG 52), *Mobile Bay* (CG 53), 54, 55 and 56 to be built by Ingalls, while Bath Iron Works, selected as the second source contractor, will be responsible for *Thomas S. Gates* (CG 51), CG 59, CG 60 and CG 61. All first 16 ships should have been delivered by October 1989.

Notes: The Ticonderoga class cruisers employ the same basic hull and propulsive machinery package as that of the Spruance class destroyers, along with the same basic armament as that of the Kidd class ships. *Ticonderoga* and its sisters embody a lot of the latest composite material armour that should help ensure that the ships can accept more combat damage and still continue to function than many earlier US Navy ships. The shipboard Aegis system, which embraces the range of shipborne anti-air sensors, air defence missiles and highly automated data processing systems, enables each Ticonderoga class ship to detect, track and destroy an unprecedented number of enemy targets simultaneously. A recently quoted price for the 3-ship package covering CG 54, 55 and 56, cited by Ingalls in June 1983, was $926.129 million, or $308.7 million per fully equipped ship.

A dramatic view of USS Vincennes (*CG49*) *launching a Standard missile.*

Belknap class

USS Biddle (*CG34*) *with multi-type missile launchers forward.*

Role: General-purpose.　　　　　　　**Builders:** Various, USA.
User: US Navy.
Basic data: 7,930 tons full displacement; 547 ft (166.7 m) overall length; 54.75 ft (16.7 m) maximum beam.　　　　**Crew:** 450.
Propulsion: 2 geared steam turbines (total 85,000 shp); 2 propellers.
Sensors: 1 SPS-49 long-range air search radar; 1 SPS-48 height finder (3-D) radar; 1 SPS-10F surface search radar; 1 LN66 navigational radar; 2 SPG-53 (gun) and 2 SPG-55 (missile) fire control radars; 1 SQS-26BX bow-mounted sonar.
Armament: 1 Kaman SH-2 Seasprite helicopter; 2 quadruple Harpoon anti-ship missile launchers; 1 twin Mk 10 launcher for either Standard ER area air defence missiles or ASROC anti-submarine missiles; 1 single 5 inch Mk 42 dual-purpose gun; 1 Phalanx 20 mm air defence close-in weapons system.
Top speed: 33 knots.　　　　**Range:** 7,100 nautical miles at 20 knots.
Programme: This 9 ship class comprises; USS *Belknap* (CG26), USS *Josephus Daniels* (CG27), USS *Wainwright* (CG28), USS *Jouett* (CG29), USS *Horne* (CG30), USS *Sterett* (CG31), USS *William P. Standley* (CG32), USS *Fox* (CG33) and USS *Biddle* (CG34). All vessels were laid down between February 1962 and December 1963, entering into service between November 1964 and January 1967.
Notes: Designed as primary carrier escorts, the Belknaps are a more potently armed development of the slightly smaller Leahy class. They no longer carry the torpedo tubes initially fitted.

USS Leahy (*CG16*) *with crew in review order.*

Role: General purpose.   **Builders:** Various, USA.
User: US Navy.
Basic data: 7,880 tons full displacement; 533 ft (162.5 m) overall
length; 55 ft (16.8 m) maximum beam.   **Crew:** 405.
Propulsion: 2 geared steam turbines (total 85,000 shp); 2 propellers.
Sensors: 1 SPS-49 long-range air search radar; 1 SPS-48 height
finder (3-D) radar; 1 SPS-10 surface search and navigational radar; 4
SPG-55B missile fire control radars; 1 SQS-23 bow-mounted sonar;
NTDS automated action information data processing system.
Armament: 2 twin Mk 10 launchers for Terrier/Standard ER area air
defence missiles; Harpoon anti-ship missiles being fitted in place of
original 2 twin 3 inch guns amidships; 1 octuple ASROC anti-sub-
marine missile launcher; 2 triple lightweight anti-submarine torpedo
tubes. Helicopter pad only.
Top speed: 32 knots.   **Range:** 8,000 nautical miles at 14 knots.
Programme: This 9 ship class comprises; USS *Leahy* (CG16), USS
Harry E. Yarnell (CG17), USS *Worden* (CG18), USS *Dale* (CG19),
USS *Richmond K. Turner* (CG20), USS *Gridley* (CG21), USS *England* (CG22), USS *Halsey* (CG23) and USS *Reeves* (CG24). All were
commissioned between August 1962 and June 1964. Last major refit
commenced during 1976.
Notes: The smallest of the US cruiser classes, the Leahys, as with
other US warships, are being equipped with 2 Phalanx 20 mm close-
in weapons systems to help fend off air attack.

Kresta II class   Cruisers

Admiral Isakov, *second of this ten ship class.*

Role: Anti-submarine.   **Builder:** Zhdanov, USSR.
User: Soviet Navy.
Basic data: 7,600 tons full displacement; 524 ft (160 m) overall length; 55,75 ft (17 m) maximum beam.   **Crew:** 380.
Propulsion: Steam turbines (total 100,000 shp); 2 propellers.
Sensors: 1 long-range air search radar; 1 height finder radar, 2 sea search and navigational radars; 4 fire control radars (2 each for missile and gun systems); 1 hull-mounted sonar.
Armament: 1 Kamov Ka-25 helicopter; 2 quadruple SS-N-14 anti-submarine missile launchers; 2 twin SA-N-3 surface-to-air missile launchers; 2 twin 57 mm and 4 Gatling 30 mm anti-aircraft guns; 2 multi-barrel anti-submarine rocket launchers; 10 torpedo tubes.
Top speed: 35 knots.   **Range:** 7,000 nautical miles at 14 knots.
Programme: All 10 ships of this class were delivered between 1970 and 1978, comprising; *Kronshtadt* (1970), *Admiral Isakov* (1971), *Admiral Nakimov* (1972), *Admiral Marakov* (1973), *Marshall Voroshilov* (1973), *Admiral Oktyabr'skiy* (1974), *Admiral Isachenkov* (1975), *Marshal Timosenko* (1976), *Vasiliy Chapaev* (1977) and *Admiral Yumashev* (1978).
Notes: Marginally longer and heavier than the Kresta Is, these ships are the first of the recent Soviet cruisers to be primarily armed for anti-submarine duties. Note the heavy SA-N-3 area air defence capability effective out to 30 nautical miles.

Kresta I class

Cruisers

A Soviet Navy Kresta I class cruising out of the Black Sea.

Role: Anti-ship.
User: Soviet Navy.
Builder: Zhdanov, USSR.
Basic data: 7,500 tons full displacement; 508.5 ft (155.0 m) overall length; 55.8 ft (170 m) maximum beam.
Crew: 380.
Propulsion: 2 geared steam turbines (total 100,000 shp); 2 propellers.
Sensors: 1 each of 2 separate long-range air search radars; 2 sea search and navigational radars; 2 and 1 of two separate fire control radars for SS-N-3 missiles; 2 fire control radars for SA-N-1 missiles; 2 fire control radars for 57 mm guns; 1 IFF radar; 1 hull-mounted sonar; automated action information data processing; data links.
Armament: 1 Kamov Ka-26 helicopter; 2 twin SS-N-3 'Shaddock' anti-ship missile launchers; 2 twin SA-N-1 'Goa' area air defence missile launchers; 2 twin 57 mm anti-aircraft guns; 2 twelve-barrelled 250 mm RBU-6000 and 2 six-barrelled 450 mm RBU-1000 anti-submarine rocket launchers; 2 quintuple heavyweight anti-submarine torpedo tubes.
Top speed: 32 knots.
Range: 7,000 nautical miles at 14 knots.
Programme: This 4-ship class comprises; *Vitse Admiral Drozd, Sevastopol, Admiral Zozulya* and *Vladivostok*. Two ships each were launched in 1965 and 1966, with two each entering service in 1966 and 1967, respectively.
Notes: Still primarily orientated towards the anti-ship mission as was the preceding Kynda class of cruisers, the Kresta 1 class ships were heavier than their forebears, reflecting their heavier and better balanced weapons fit. The Kresta 1 class were the first Soviet cruiser to be fitted with a helicopter hangar and are reported to be refitted with 4 single 30 mm Gatling type close-in weapons systems.

Andrea Doria class   Cruisers

Andrea Doria (*C 553*). *Note the hardly visible forward funnel.*

Role: Anti-aircraft.   **Builder:** CNR, Italy.
User: Italian Navy.
Basic data: 6,412 tons full displacement; 489.8 ft (149.3 m) overall length; 56.4 ft (17.2 m) maximum beam.   **Crew:** 514.
Propulsion: 2 CNR-built De Laval geared steam turbines (total 60,000 shp); 2 propellers.
Sensors: 1 SPS-52B air search/height finder (3-D) radar; 1 Selenia/Elsag RAN-20S low-level air search and tracking radar; 1 SMA SPQ-2D surface search and navigational radar; 2 SPG-55C missile fire control radars; 4 Selenia/Elsag RTN-10X missile/gun fire control radars; 1 SQS-23 hull-mounted sonar. Selenia automated action information data processing.
Armament: 4 Augusta-Bell AB 212ASW helicopters (2 only on C554); 1 twin Mk 10 launcher for Standard area air defence missiles; 8 single 76 mm OTO-Melara anti-aircraft guns (6 only on C554); 2 triple Elsag Mk 32 lightweight anti-submarine torpedo tubes.
Top speed: 32 knots.   **Range:** 5,210 nautical miles at 20 knots.
Programme: This 2 ship class comprises: *Andrea Doria* (C553) and *Caio Duilio* (C554). *Andrea Doria* entered service in February 1964, followed by its sister ship in November 1964. Both cruisers underwent major refits during the latter 1970s. During this refit, *Caio Duilio* was converted into a training cruiser, having its aft pair of pedestal-mounted 76 mm guns removed in order to lengthen and heighten the former hangar, now used as a school and living quarters for trainees.
Notes: Besides shipping a powerful anti-air capability, the spacious helipad aft ensures that the ships can make a material contribution when operating against a submarine threat.

Kynda class   Cruisers

Groznyy *transitting the North Sea, April 1984.*

Role: Anti-ship.   **Builder:** Zhdanov, USSR.
User: Soviet Navy.
Basic data: 5,600 tons full displacement; 459 ft (140 m) overall length; 51.8 ft (15.8 m) maximum beam.   **Crew:** 375.
Propulsion: 2 geared steam turbines (total 100,000 shp); 2 propellers.
Sensors: 2 long-range air search radars; 2 sea search and navigational radars; 2 tracking radars (SS-N-3); 1 tracking radar (both missile systems); 2 tracking radars (SA-N-1); 1 hull-mounted sonar.
Armament: 2 quadruple SS-N-3 'Shaddrock' anti-ship cruise missile launchers; 1 twin SA-N-1 'Goa' medium-range anti-aircraft missile launcher; 2 twin 76 mm dual-purpose guns; 2 triple heavyweight anti-submarine torpedo tubes; 2 twelve barrel 250 mm RBU6000 anti-submarine rocket launchers. Helipad aft but no helicopter.
Top speed: 34 knots.   **Range:** 6,800 nautical miles at 15 knots.
Programme: The first of this 4 ship class was laid down in June 1960, with the first two, *Groznyy* and *Admiral Fukin*, entering service with the Soviet fleet in 1962, followed by *Admiral Golovko* and *Varyag* in 1965.
Notes: The first of the modern breed of Soviet guided missile carrying cruisers, these relatively light ships pack a potent primary armament of 16 'Shaddrock' anti-ship cruise missiles (including reloads), capable of delivering a nuclear or conventional warhead over a range of around 250 nautical miles (463 km). Besides the area air defence missiles, the Kynda class carries a fairly heavy onboard sub-surface punch in the form of its anti-submarine torpedoes and the complement of up to 3.2 nautical mile (6 km) ranging anti-submarine rockets.

Udaloy class   Destroyers

Udaloy *showing the ship's highly raked clipper bow and generally busy upper profile surmounting a clean, seaworthy-looking hull.*

Role: Anti-submarine.   **Builders**: Various, USSR.
User: Soviet Navy.
Basic data: 8,200 tons full displacement; 531 ft (162.0 m) overall length; 63.3 ft (19.3 m) maximum beam.   **Crew**: c 300.
Propulsion: 4 gas turbines (total 120,000 shp); COGAG; 2 propellers.
Sensors: 2 air search and height finder (3-D) radars; 3 low-level air/sea search radars; 2 each fire control radars for anti-submarine missile and air defence missile systems; 1 fire control radar for 100 mm guns; 2 fire control radars for 30 mm guns; 1 bow-mounted sonar; 1 towed variable depth sonar; automated action information data processing system and long range (satellite) data links.
Armament: 2 Kamov Ka-26 'Hormone' or Ka-27 'Helix' helicopters; 2 quadruple SS-N-14 anti-submarine missile launchers; 8 vertically-launched SA-NX-8 air defence missiles; 2 single 100 mm dual-purpose guns; 4 single 30 mm Gatling-type anti-aircraft guns; 2 twelve-barrel 250 mm RBU-6000 anti-submarine rocket launchers; 2 quadruple heavyweight anti-submarine torpedo tubes; mines.
Top speed: 33 knots.
Range: 6,000 nautical miles at 20 knots (estimated).
Programme: Believed to be the precursor of a large class, the first 2 ships, *Udaloy* and *Vitse Admiral Kulikov*, were laid down during 1978 in the Kalingrad and Zhdanov shipyards, respectively, followed by 2 more in 1979. *Udaloy*, the lead ship, commenced sea trials in the Baltic in November 1980 and the *Vitse Admiral Kulikov* went to sea in 1982.
Notes: Designed as a replacement for the earlier Krivak class anti-submarine frigates, the Udaloy class consists of much larger and heavier ships, being in many ways directly comparable to the US Navy's Spruance class destroyers. As with the Spruance class, the Udaloys

carry a very respectable secondary anti-air sensor/weapons fit. The ship's primary armament of eight 25 nautical mile ranging SS-N-14 anti-submarine missiles are mounted, as with the Kara and Kresta II classes, in 2 quadruple 'bin' launchers immediately below the ship's bridge. The 8 silos for the new, vertically launched SA-NX-8 air defence missiles are reported to be dispersed about the ship: 4 being housed under a large hatch in the bow section, the other two twin missile silos being mounted in tandem immediately forward of the helicopter hangar structure. The ship's 2 single 100mm guns are fully automatic and are reported to have an 80 rounds per minute maximum rate of fire. The four 30mm Gatling-type rapid-fire anti-aircraft guns are placed above the corners of the raised main hull section amidships, from where each has a totally unobstructed hemispherical arc of fire. The Udaloys' two 12-barrelled RBU-6000 anti-submarine rocket launchers are mounted on either side of the forward part of the helicopter hangar superstructure: the quadruple 533mm anti-submarine torpedo launchers each being mounted at the sides of the forward end of the low deck. As with other Soviet warships, the Udaloys' upper hull sections are pockmarked with readily openable portholes; a practice frowned upon in the West for many years now, as part of the steps deemed necessary to 'close the ship down' so as to minimise inward seepages when operating in a chemical/bacteriological/nuclear warfare environment.

An abeam view of the Udaloy class destroyer.

Sovremennyy class   Destroyers

The weapons layout of the Sovremennyy class is clearly visible from this angle.

Role: General-purpose.   **Builder:** Zhdanov, Leningrad, USSR.
User: Soviet Navy.
Basic data: 8,075 tons full displacement; 510.5 ft (155.6 m) overall length; 57.1 ft (17.4 m) maximum beam.   **Crew:** 330.
Propulsion: 2 geared steam turbines (total 110,000 shp); 2 propellers.
Sensors: 1 long range air search and height finder (3-D) radar; 3 sea search and navigational radars; 6 fire control radars for SA-N-7 missiles; 1 fire control radar for 130 mm guns; 2 fire control radars for 30 mm guns; 1 bow-mounted sonar; automated action-information system and long range (satellite) data link.
Armament: 1 Kamo Ka-26 'Hormone B' helicopter; 2 quadruple SS-N-9 'Siren' anti-ship cruise missile launchers; 2 single SA-N-7 medium ranged air defence missile launchers; 2 twin 130 mm dual-purpose guns; 4 single 30 mm Gatling-type anti-aircraft guns; 2 twin 533 mm heavyweight anti-submarine torpedo tubes; 2 six-barrel 450 mm RBU-1000 anti-submarine rocket launchers ; mines.
Top speed: 33 knots.   **Range:** 6,500 nautical miles at 18 knots.
Programme: Currently building at about one per year, the lead ship, *Sovremennyy*, was reported to have been laid down during 1976 and entered sea trials in the summer of 1980 before joining the Northern Fleet in late 1981. The 2nd of class, *Otchavanij*, laid down in 1977, entered trials in May 1982. A 3rd and 4th of class are reported to have been laid down in 1978 and 1979, respectively. In all, 5 of these ships had been launched by the end of 1983.
Notes: The Sovremennyy class design employs the same basic hull

and propulsion machinery as the Kresta I and II classes but incorporates a more up-to-date armament fit on a radically altered superstructure. The Sovremennyy class carries the SS-N-9 'Siren' anti-ship cruise missile with a range of up to 60 nautical miles (111 km), the missiles being housed in large cannister-type quadruple launchers mounted on the main deck on either side of the bridge structure. The 2 single SA-N-7 air defence missile launchers are mounted on the raised deck areas immediately aft of the forward 130 mm gun and the helipad, respectively. With a range of up to 15.1 nautical miles (28 km), the SA-N-7 installations with their nearby missile reload magazines give the ship a healthy anti-air capability, supported by the new, water-cooled 130 mm guns and 30 mm rapid-fire close-in anti-sea skimmer missile weapons. As with the other most recent classes of Soviet warships, this class carries 4 of these six-barrelled 30 mm close-in weapons positioned on either flank of the ship immediately forward of the bridge and just aft of the retracted telescopic hangar (quite clearly the Soviets had respect for the incoming low-level air threat long before the Falklands experience brought the lesson home). The fully automatic 130 mm guns, with their effective range of 8.1 nautical miles (15 km), should provide the ship with not only a useful secondary anti-ship punch, but be useful in terms of ship-to-shore bombardment.

A forward aspect of Sovremennyy, *1981.*

Spruance class

Destroyers

USS Fletcher (*DDG992*) *prior to installation of Phalanx weapons.*

Role: Anti-submarine.   **Builder:** Ingalls Shipbuilding, USA.
User: US Navy.
Basic data: 7,800 tons full displacement; 563.3 ft (171.7 m) overall
length, 55 ft (16.8 m) maximum beam.   **Crew:** 302.
Propulsion: 4 General Electric LM2500 gas turbines (total
80,000 shp); COGAG; 2 controllable-pitch propellers.
Sensors: 1 SPS-40B air search radar; 1 SPS-55 surface search radar;
1 SPG-60 STIR missile fire control radar; 1 SPQ-9A surface target fire
control radar; 1 SQS-53 bow-mounted sonar; NTDS automated action
information data processing system.
Armament: 1 Sikorsky SH-3 Sea King or 2 Sikorsky SH-60 Seahawk
helicopters; 1 octuple Mk 29 launcher for Sea Sparrow point air defence missiles; 2 quadruple Harpoon anti-ship missile launchers; 2
single 5 inch Mk 45 dual-purpose guns; 2 Phalanx 20 mm close-in
weapons systems; 1 octuple Mk 16 launcher for ASROC anti-submarine missiles.
Top speed: 32 knots.   **Range:** 6,000 nautical miles at 20 knots.
Programme: The 31 ship Spruance class destroyers were subject of
a sole source contract placed with the Ingalls Shipbuilding Divison of
Litton Industries in June 1970 (for 30 ships, 1 being added in Septem-
ber 1979). The class comprises: USS *Spruance* (DD963), USS *Paul
F. Foster* (DD964), USS *Kinkaid* (DD965), USS *Hewitt* (DD966),
USS *Elliott* (DD967), USS *Arthur W. Radford* (DD968), USS *Peterson*
(DD969), USS *Caron* (DD970), USS *David R. Ray* (DD971), USS
Oldendorf (DD972), USS *John Young* (DD973), USS *Comte de
Grasse* (DD974), USS *O'Brien* (DD975), USS *Merrill* (DD976), USS
Briscoe (DD977), USS *Stump* (DD978), USS *Conolly* (DD979),
USS *Moosbrugger* (DD980), USS *John Hancock* (DD981), USS
Nicholson (DD982), USS *John Rodgers* (DD983), USS *Leftwich*

(DD984), USS *Cushing* (DD985), USS *Harry W. Hill* (DD986), USS *O'Bannon* (DD987), USS *Thorn* (DD988), USS *Deyo* (DD989), USS *Ingersoll* (DD990), USS *Fife* (DD991), USS *Fletcher* (DD992) and USS *Hayler* (DD997). With the exception of the lately ordered 31st ship, all Spruances were laid down between November 1972 and April 1978 and all 30 were commissioned between September 1975 and July 1980; with the 31st ship, *Hayler*, commissioning in March 1983. (The 4 ships, DD993 through DD996, were anti-air versions of the Spruance ordered by Iran, but subsequently brought into US Navy service as the Kidd class.)

Notes: Large and very angular of line, the Spruance class ships were built as replacements for the World War II destroyers of the Allen M. Sumner and Gearing classes. Designed using modular construction techniques, the Spruance class ships employ a COmbined Gas And Gas (COGAG) machinery arrangement in which the vessel can be propelled by one, two, three or all four LM2500 engines . In the Spruances, the ship's main machinery of 4 gas turbines is grouped into two physically separated engine rooms (to minimise potential battle damage) and this, in turn, leads to the rather unusual asymmetric staggering of the ships' funnels, or stacks, as they are called, the forward one being set to port, aft to starboard. All are being retrofitted with 2 Phalanx 20 mm systems.

USS Fife *(DDG991), December 1982.*

Shirane class   Destroyers

Japan's Shirane *(DDH143). Note the lengthy helipad aft.*

Role: Anti-submarine.
Builder: Ishikawajima Heavy Industries, Japan.
User: Japanese Maritime Self-Defence Force.
Basic data: 6,800 tons full displacement; 521.0 ft (158.8 m) overall length; 57.4 ft (17.5 m) maximum beam.   **Crew:** 370.
Propulsion: 2 geared steam turbines (total 70,000 shp); 2 propellers.
Sensors: 1 OPS 12 long range air search and height finder (3-D) radar; 1 OPS 28 sea search and navigational radar; 1 Hollandse WM 25 fire control radar (for Sea Sparrow); 2 GFCS 1A gun fire control radars; 1 TACAN aircraft homer; 1 OQS 100 bow-mounted sonar; 1 SQS-35 variable depth sonar; 1 SQS-18A passive towed array sonar; naval tactical information data processing system.
Armament: 3 Kawasaki-built SH-3 Sea King helicopters; 2 single 5 inch Mk 42 dual-purpose guns; 1 octuple Mk 20 launcher for Sea Sparrow point air defence missiles; 1 octuple launcher for ASROC anti-submarine missiles; 2 triple lightweight anti-submarine torpedo tubes; 2 Phalanx 20 mm close-in weapons systems.
Top speed: 32 knots.   **Endurance:** Over 6,000 nautical miles.
Programme: Authorised for construction in 1976, this 2 ship class comprises; *Shirane* (DDG143) and *Kurama* (DDG144). The *Shirane* entered service in March 1980. *Kurama* joined the Japanese fleet in March 1981.
Notes: The Shirane class design is based on that of the earlier Haruna class, using the same propulsive machinery married to a slightly longer hull. Better armed than the Haruna class, these Shirane class destroyers have a very impressive anti-submarine capability and once fitted with Harpoon anti-ship missiles, as is planned, will pack a useful anti-ship punch too.

Bristol type   Destroyers

HMS Bristol *(D23). Note the unusual side-by-side positioning of the ship's 2 aft funnels.*

Role: Area air defence.   **Builder:** Swan Hunter, UK.
User: Royal Navy.
Basic data: 6,750 tons displacement; 507.0 ft (154.5 m) overall length; 55.0 ft (16.8 m) maximum beam.   **Crew:** 407.
Propulsion: 2 Rolls-Royce TM-1A Olympus gas turbines (total 44,000 shp); 2 GEC geared steam turbines (total 30,000 shp); COSAG; 2 propellers.
Sensors: 1 Type 965M long range air search radar with IFF; 1 Type 992Q low altitude air search radar; 2 Type 909 fire control radars for Sea Dart; 2 fire control radars for Ikara; 1 Type 1006 navigational radar; 1 each of Types 162, 170, 182, 184 and 189 hull-mounted sonars; Ferranti ADAWS 2 automated action information data system.
Armament: 1 twin Sea Dart area air defence missile launcher; 1 single 4.5 inch Vickers Mk 8 dual-purpose gun; 1 single Ikara anti-submarine missile launcher; 1 triple-barrel Mk 10 Limbo anti-submarine mortar; 2 single 20 mm anti-aircraft guns; aft helipad for up to Lynx-sized helicopter but no hangar.
Top speed: 32 knots.   **Range:** 5,000 nautical miles at 18 knots.
Programme: Initially planned as a 4 ship class of which only HMS *Bristol* (D23) was authorised for building in 1966. HMS *Bristol* commissioned in March 1973.
Notes: Designed as a successor to the County class destroyers, the primary function of the Bristol, or Type 82 ships, was to have given air defence screening for the Royal Navy's planned 50,000 ton CVA aircraft carrier.

Haruna class   Destroyers

The Mitsubishi-built Haruna *(DDH141), with Sea King helipad aft.*

Range: Anti-submarine.   **Builders:** Mitsubishi and IHI, Japan.
User: Japanese Maritime Self-Defence Force.
Basic data: 6,300 tons full displacement; 502 ft (153 m) overall length; 57.4 ft (17.5 m) maximum beam.   **Crew:** 340.
Propulsion: 2 geared steam turbines (total 70,000 shp); 2 propellers.
Sensors: 1 OPS 11 long-range air search radar; 1 OPS 17 sea search and navigational radar; 2 GFCS 1 fire control radars; 1 OQS 3 hull-mounted sonar; 1 URN-20A TACAN aircraft homer; automated naval tactical information data processing system.
Armament: 3 Kawasaki-built SH-3 Sea King helicopters; 2 single 5 inch Mk 42 dual-purpose guns; 1 octuple Mk 16 launcher for ASROC anti-submarine missiles (1 Mk 25 launcher for Sea Sparrow point air defence missiles being retrofitted to both ships during early 1980s refits, along with Phalanx).
Top speed: 32 knots.   **Endurance:** Over 7,000 nautical miles.
Programme: *Haruna* (DDH141), the lead destroyer of this 2 ship class, was built by Mitsubishi, while *Hiei* (DDH142) was constructed by IHI. The ships entered service in March 1973 and December 1974, respectively.
Notes: Large, fast ships, the Haruna class design, with its capability to deploy no less than 3 Sea King submarine-hunting helicopters, clearly added a broader dimension to Japan's naval anti-submarine forces.

HMS Norfolk (*D21*), *prior to becoming* Captain Prat.

Role: Anti-aircraft.   **Builders:** Various, UK.
Users: Royal Navy , Chilean Navy, Pakistan Navy.
Basic data: 6,200 tons full displacement; 520 ft (158.5 m) overall
length; 54 ft (16.5 m) maximum beam.   **Crew:** 486.
Propulsion: 2 AEI geared steam turbines (total 30,000 shp) plus 4
Metrovick G.6 gas turbines (total 30,000 shp); COSAG; 2 propellers.
Sensors: 1 Type 965 long-range air search radar; 1 Type 992Q low-
level air and surface search radar; 1 Type 278 height finder (3-D) radar;
1 Type 901 Seaslug fire control radar; 1 Type 903 gun fire control
radar; 2 Type 904 Seacat fire control radars; 1 Type 1006 sea search
and navigational radar; 1 Type 184 hull-mounted sonar; ADAWS 1
automated action information data processing system.
Armament: 2 Westland Wessex helicopters; 1 twin Mk II launcher for
Seaslug area air defence missiles; 4 Exocet anti-ship missiles on D18,
D19, D20 and D21, which replaces the 'B' or 2nd gun turret, other
ships carrying 2 twin 4.5 inch Mk 6 dual-purpose guns; 2 quadruple
Seacat point air defence missile launchers.
Top speed: 30 knots.   **Range:** 3,500 nautical miles at 28 knots.
Programme: Originally an 8 ship class built between March 1959
and October 1970, HMS *Glamorgan* (D19) and HMS *Fife* (D20) remain in service with the Royal Navy, while the former HMS *Norfolk*
(D21) and *Antrim* (D18) have been sold to the Chilean Navy where
they serve as the *Capitan Prat* and *Almirante Cochrane*. Another ship,
the former HMS *London* (D16), has been sold to Pakistan, where it
serves as the *Babur*.
Notes: Sturdy ships, HMS *Glamorgan* survived an Exocet strike while
operating in the Falklands with her sister, HMS *Antrim*.

Suffren class   Destroyers

Duquesne (*D603*) *underway in the Atlantic, 1977.*

Role: General purpose.   **Builders:** DCAN (various), France.
User: French Navy.
Basic data: 6,090 tons full displacement; 517 ft (157.6 m) overall
length; 50.85 ft (15.5 m) maximum beam.   **Crew:** 355.
Propulsion: 2 Rateau geared steam turbines (total 72,500 shp); 2
propellers.
Sensors: 1 DRBI 23 air search (3-D) radar; 1 DRBV 50 surface search
radar; 1 Decca/DRBN 32 sea search and navigational radar; 2 DRBR
51 fire control radars (Masurca); DRBC 32A fire control radar (100 mm
guns); 1 DUBV 23 hull-mounted sonar; 1 DUBV 43 towed variable
depth sonar; SENIT automated action information data processor.
Armament: 4 Exocet anti-ship missile launchers; 1 twin Masurca
area air defence missile launcher (reloadable); 1 Malafon anti-submarine missile launcher (13 missiles); 2 100 mm Model 1968 dual-purpose
guns; 4 single 20 mm Oerlikon anti-aircraft guns; 2 heavyweight anti-
submarine torpedo catapults (10 torpedoes).
Top speed: 34 knots.   **Range:** 5,100 nautical miles at 18 knots.
Programme: A 2 ship class, the first, *Suffren* (D602), was laid down
in December 1962 and accepted in July 1967. *Duquesne* (D603)
being accepted in April 1970.
Notes: Belonging to the first generation of guided missile destroyers,
the two Suffren class ships lack the anti-submarine reach provided by
carrying a helicopter.

Tourville class

Tourville (*D610*) *at speed in the Bay of Biscay.*

Role: Anti-submarine.   **Builder:** DCAN Lorient, France.
User: French Navy.
Basic data: 5,700 tons full displacement; 500.3 ft (152.5 m) overall length; 50.2 ft (15.3 m) maximum beam.   **Crew:** 282.
Propulsion: 2 Rateau geared steam turbines (total 57,300 shp); 2 propellers.
Sensors: 1 DRBV 26 long-range air search radar; 1 DRBV 51 B low-level air and surface search radar; 1 DRBC 32D gun fire control radar; 2 Decca 1226 sea search and navigational radars; 1 DUBV 23 bow-mounted sonar, used in conjunction with 1 DUBV 43 towed, variable depth sonar; SENIT 3 automated action information data processing system.
Armament: 2 Westland Lynx helicopters; 6 Exocet anti-ship missile launchers; 2 single 100 mm Model 1968 dual-purpose guns; 1 Crotale point air defence missile launcher system; 2 single 20 mm Oerlikon anti-aircraft guns; 1 single Malafon anti-submarine missile launcher; 2 heavyweight anti-submarine torpedo catapults.
Top speed: 31 knots.   **Endurance:** In excess of 6,000 nautical miles.
Programme: This 3 ship class comprises *Tourville* (D610), *Duguay Trouin* (D611) and *De Grasse* (D612). Laid down between 1970 and 1972, the ships entered service in June 1974, September 1975 and October 1977, respectively. The rapid-response Crotale was recently installed in place of the aft (third) 100 mm gun shown in the photograph. All three ships are planned to remain in service until the year 2000.
Notes: This class is a more compact, well armed development of the earlier Suffren class.

Modified Kashin/Kashin class   Destroyers

A Modified Kashin operating in the Mediterranean, May 1979.

Role: General purpose.   **Builders:** Various, USSR.
Users: Soviet and Indian Navies.
Basic data: c 4,850 tons full displacement; 479 ft (146 m) overall length; 51.85 ft (15.8 m) maximum beam.   **Crew:** 280.
Propulsion: 4 gas turbines (total 96,000 shp); 2 propellers.
Sensors: 1 long-range air search radar; 2 height finder (3-D) radars; 2 sea search and navigational radars; 4 fire control radars consisting of 2 separate systems; 1 hull-mounted sonar; 1 towed variable depth sonar (on Modified Kashins only).
Armament: 4 single SS-N-2 anti-ship missile launchers (Modified Kashins only); 2 twin SA-N-1 point air defence missile launchers; 2 twin 76 mm anti-aircraft guns; 4 single Gatling-type 30 mm anti-aircraft guns (Modified Kashins only); 5 heavyweight anti-submarine torpedo tubes; 2 twelve-barrel RB 6000 anti-submarine 250 mm rocket launchers (on all Kashins and on at least 1 Modified Kashin).
Top speed: 36 knots.   **Range:** 5,000 nautical miles at 18 knots.
Programme: 20 Kashin class ships were constructed between 1962 and 1972 and 5 of these ships were known to have been converted to Modified Kashins commencing 1973. One Kashin sank in the Black Sea in August 1974 following an internal explosion. The Indian Government operate Modified Kashins; the three ships being, *Rajput* (D51), *Rana* (D52) and *Ranjit* (D53).
Notes: The Kashin class guided missile destroyers were the first large gas-turbine powered ships to emerge anywhere in the world. Modified Kashins have an enlarged and elevated helicopter pad aft for a single Kamov Ka-25.

Tachikaze class

Destroyers

Asakaze (*D169*) *photographed at speed in 1979.*

Role: Anti-aircraft.   **Builder:** Mitsubishi, Japan.
User: Japanese Maritime Self-Defence Force.
Basic data: 4,800 tons full displacement; 469.2 ft (143 m) overall length; 46.9 ft (14.3 m) maximum beam.   **Crew:** 277.
Propulsion: 2 geared steam turbines (total 70,000 shp); 2 propellers.
Sensors: 1 OPS-17 sea search and navigational radar; 1 SPS-52B height finder (3-D) radar; 2 SPG-51 missile fire control radar; 1 GFCS 1 gun fire control radar; 1 OQS-3 hull-mounted sonar, automated action information data processing system.
Armament: 1 single Mk 13 launcher for Standard SM-1 MR area air defence missiles; 2 single 5 inch Mk 42 dual-purpose guns; 1 octuple ASROC anti-submarine missile launcher; 2 triple lightweight anti-submarine torpedo tubes.
Top speed: 32 knots. **Endurance:** In excess of 4,000 nautical miles.
Programme: This 3 ship class comprises *Tachikaze* (D168), *Asakaze* (D169) and *Sawakaze* (D170). Laid down in 1973, 1976 and 1979, the three ships entered service in March 1976, March 1979 and March 1983.
Notes: Employing the same propulsive machinery as the somewhat heavier Haruna class destroyers, the Tachikaze class, along with the single Amatsukaze type destroyer, were the first Japanese warships to carry an area air defence capability. No helicopter is carried.

Type 42 class   Destroyers

The Vosper Thornycroft-built Batch III ship HMS Gloucester *(D95).*

Role: Area air defence.   **Builders:** Various, UK and Argentina.
Users: Royal Navy and Argentinian Navy.

Basic data:	Batch I and II	Batch III
Full displacement:	4,250 tons	4,700 tons
Overall length:	410 ft (125 m)	463 ft (141.1 m)
Maximum beam:	47 ft (14.3 m)	49 ft (14.9 m)
Crew:	280	301

Propulsion: 2 Rolls-Royce TM3B Olympus gas turbines (total 54,400 shp); 2 Rolls-Royce Tyne RM1A in Batch I or Tyne RM1C in Batches II and III (total 7,600 or 10,680 shp); COGOG; 2 controllable-pitch propellers.
Sensors: 1 type 965M (Batch I) or 1 Type 1022 (Batches II and III) long range air search radar and IFF; 1 Type 992Q low altitude air search radar; 1 Type 1006 sea search and navigational radar; 2 Type 909 fire control radars for Sea Dart; Types 162, 170B, 174 and 184 hull-mounted sonars; Ferranti ADAWS 4 automated action information data processing system; long range (satellite) data links.
Armament: 1 Westland Lynx helicopter; 1 twin Mk 30 Sea Dart area air defence missile launcher; 1 single 4.5 inch Vickers Mk 8 dual-purpose gun; 2 twin 30 mm and 2 single 20 mm Oerlikon anti-aircraft guns; 2 triple lightweight anti-submarine torpedo tubes; 2 rapid-fire 30 mm close-in gun weapons systems to be retrofitted.
Top speed: 28 knots (Batch I and II) or 30 knots (Batch III).
Range: 4,500 (Batch I and II) or 4,750 nautical miles (Batch III) at 18 knots.
Programme: Originally destined to be a 16 ship class, of which 2 have been lost, the Type 42 or Sheffield class comprises 8 Batch I vessels, 4 Batch II and 4 Batch III examples of the Stretched Type 42. The Royal Navy Batch I ships, along with their commissioning dates are: HMS *Sheffield* (D80), February 1975; HMS *Birmingham* (D86), December 1976; HMS *Coventry* (D118), November 1978; HMS

Cardiff (D108), October 1979; HMS *Newcastle* (D87), March 1978 and HMS *Glasgow* (D88), May 1979. The two Argentinian ships (also Batch I) are *Hercules* (D28), July 1976 and *Santisima Trinidad* (D29), 1981. The Batch IIs are; HMS *Exeter* (D89), September 1980; HMS *Southampton* (D90), July 1981; HMS *Nottingham* (D91), April 1983 and HMS *Liverpool* (D92), July 1982. The Batch III Stretched Type 42s comprise: HMS *Manchester* (D95), December 1982, along with HMS *Gloucester* (D96), HMS *Edinburgh* (D97) and HMS *York* (D98), all in service by the end of 1985. Vickers acted as the lead yard with the building programme spread over 5 yards comprising: Vickers—D80, D28, D108 and D95; Cammell Laird—D86, D118, D92 and D97; Swan Hunter—D87, D88, D89 and D98; Vosper Thornycroft—D90, D91 and D96, with the Argentinian AFNE naval yard responsible for D29. Both HMS *Sheffield* and HMS *Coventry* were lost to enemy action in May 1982.

Notes: Designed as replacement for the County class destroyers, the Sheffield class, or Type 42s, are much more compact and austere ships than their forebears. The primary role of the Type 42s is to provide area air defence for the ships that they are accompanying. Regrettably, as the loss of HMS *Sheffield* and HMS *Coventry* showed, the latterday type of hull construction is relatively fragile making the ships vulnerable to low-level air attack from sea-skimming missiles in the case of HMS *Sheffield*, or streamed manned aircraft, as in the case of the sinking of HMS *Coventry*. Her Majesty's ships *Cardiff*, *Glasgow* and *Exeter* also saw action in the Falklands theatre, *Glasgow* surviving a direct hit in its main engine space by a bomb that, fortunately, failed to explode.

The final Batch I, HMS Glasgow (*D88*).

Kanin class   Destroyers

A Kanin class revealing much of her generally low profile.

Role: Anti-aircraft.
Builders: Zhdanov, Severodvinsk and Kommuna, USSR.
User: Soviet Navy.
Basic data: 4,700 tons full displacement; 462.6 ft (141.0 m) overall
length; 47.9 ft (14.6 m) maximum beam.   **Crew:** 300.
Propulsion: 2 geared steam turbines (total 80,000 shp); 2 propellers.
Sensors: 1 long range air search radar; 1 IFF radar; 2 sea search and
navigational radars; 3 separate types of fire control radars (1 each for
missiles, 57 mm and 30 mm guns); 1 hull-mounted sonar; naval tactical
information system.
Armament: 1 twin SA-N-1 'Goa' area air defence missile launcher;
2 quadruple 57 mm and 4 twin 30 mm anti-aircraft guns; 3 twelve-
barrelled 250 mm RBU-6000 anti-submarine rocket launchers; 2
quintuple heavyweight anti-submarine torpedo tubes.
Top speed: 34 knots.   **Range:** 4,500 nautical miles at 18 knots.
Programme: The Kanin class comprises 8 converted Krupnyy class
destroyers, these modernised missile-carrying conversions entering
service between 1958 and 1960. The Kanin class ship names are:
Boykiy, Derzkiy, Gnevnyy, Gordyy, Gremyashchiy, Upornyy, Zhguchiy
and *Zorkiy.*
Notes: Almost direct contemporaries of the US Navy's Charles F.
Adams class, the Kanin class was slightly faster despite its greater
weight, but lacked the bigger gunned anti-ship punch of its US
rivals. This Soviet class will probably be retired before the close of the
1980s.

Audace class   Destroyers

Italy's Audace *(D551) guided missile destroyer.*

Role: Anti-submarine.   **Builders:** Various, Italy.
User: Italian Navy.
Basic data: 4,554 tons full displacement; 469.2 ft (143.0 m) overall
length; 47.9 ft (14.6 m) maximum beam.   **Crew:** 380.
Propulsion: 2 CNR or Ansoldo geared steam turbines (total
73,000 shp); 2 propellers.
Sensors: 1 SPS-12 long-range air search radar; 1 SPQ-2 combined
air/sea search radar; 1 SPS-52 height finder (3-D) radar; 1 sea search
and navigational radar; 2 SPG-518 fire control radars (missile); 3
Selenia RTN-10X fire control radars (guns); 1 CWE 610 hull-
mounted sonar; naval tactical data system.
Armament: 3 AB 204/212-sized or 2 SH-3-sized helicopters; 1 single
launcher for Standard SM-1 area air defence missiles; 2 single OTO-
Melara 127 mm dual-purpose guns; 4 single OTO-Melara 76 mm-air-
craft guns; 2 triple and 4 single lightweight anti-submarine torpedo
tubes.
Top speed: 35.2 knots.   **Range:** 4,000 nautical miles at 25 knots.
Programme: A 2 ship class, *Ardito* (D550) and *Audace* (D551), were
ordered in 1968. Both entered service in 1972.
Notes: Extremely fast and efficient ships, the Audace class carry a
well-balanced weapons fit. The hulls of these destroyers are built of
steel, while their superstructure is built largely of light alloy. Besides
having a high top speed, the Audace class cruise at around 25 knots.

Charles F. Adams class   Destroyers

USS Waddell (*DDG24*), *last of this US Navy class.*

Role: Anti-aircraft.   **Builders:** Various, USA.
Users: US Navy, Royal Australian Navy, Federal German Navy.
Basic data: 4,550 tons full displacement; 437 ft (133.2 m) overall
length; 47 ft (14.3 m) maximum beam.   **Crew:** around 330.
Propulsion: 2 General Electric or Westinghouse geared steam turbines
(total 70,000 shp); 2 propellers.
Sensors: 1 SPS-29, -37 or -40 air search radar; 1 SPS-39 height
finder (3-D) radar; 1 SPS-10 sea search and navigational radar; 2
SPG-51C fire control radars (Standard); 1 SPG-53 fire control radar
(gun); 1 SPS-23 hull-mounted sonar.
Armament: 1 twin Mk 11 or 13 launcher for Standard area air defence
or Harpoon anti-ship missiles; 2 single 5 in Mk 42 guns; (aft gun
removed on the 3 Federal German ships to make room for 2 twin
Harpoon anti-ship missile launchers); 1 octuple ASROC anti-submarine rocket launcher (replaced by 2 Ikara anti-submarine launchers in
the 3 Australian ships); 2 triple lightweight anti-submarine torpedo
tubes.
Top speed: 31 knots.   **Range:** 4,500 nautical miles at 20 knots.
Programme: The 23 ship Charles F. Adams class was ordered for the
US Navy between mid-1957 and mid-1961, all ships being laid down
between 1958 and 1962. The lead ship, USS *Charles F. Adams*
(DDG2), built by Bath Iron Works, was followed by: USS *John King*
(3), *Lawrence* (4), *Claude V. Ricketts* (5), *Barney* (6), *Henry B. Wilson*
(7), *Lynde McCormick* (8), *Jowers* (9), *Sampson* (10), *Sellers* (11),
Robison (12), *Hoel* (13), *Buchanan* (14), *Berkeley* (15), *Joseph
Strauss* (16), *Conyngham* (17), *Semmes* (18), *Tattnal* (19), *Golds-
borough* (20), *Cochrane* (21), *Benjamin Stoddert* (22), *Richard E.
Byrd* (23) and *Waddel* (24). All of this class entered service between
September 1960 and September 1964. Australia bought 3 additional

ships, HMAS *Perth* (DDG38), HMAS *Hobart* (DDG39) and HMAS *Brisbane* (DDG41), all 3 being accepted between July 1965 and December 1967. In service with the Royal Australian Navy, these vessels are referred to as Perth class ships. During 1964, the Federal German Government placed orders for a further 3 ships of this class, *Lutjens* (D185), *Molders* (D186) and *Rommel* (D187), all of which were accepted between March 1969 and May 1970 and are operated as Lutjens class destroyers.

Notes: Slightly smaller and lighter than the Coontz class guided missile destroyers that preceded the Adams into service with the US Navy, the Adams class ships still provide around a quarter of the US Navy's total task force anti-aircraft screening capability. Currently, the US vessels are undergoing an extensive modernisation of their shipboard electronics and action information systems, along with the installation of Harpoon missile systems. Similar electronics modernisation is being carried out on the 3 Lutjens class destroyers, while within the short term, the Perth class are scheduled to be retrofitted to take Harpoon missiles. It should be noted that while the external appearance of the US and Australian ships is generally similar, the additional aft funnel-mounted mast, with its aerial arrays, helps disguise the Lutjens class ships' ancestry quite markedly. All 29 ships of this generic class carry 40 Standard SM-1 MR area air defence missiles as their primary armament, this missile being capable of ranging out to 30 nautical miles, or reaching an altitude of 60,000 feet.

USS Conyngham (*DDG17*) *in the Caribbean, 1984.*

Modified Hamburg class   Destroyers

Bayern (*D183*) *after modernisation.*

Role: General-purpose.
Builder: Blohm und Voss, Federal Germany.
User: Federal German Navy.
Basic data: 4,400 tons full displacement; 439.6 ft (134 m) overall length; 44 ft (13.4 m) maximum beam.   **Crew:** 280.
Propulsion: 2 geared steam turbines (total 68,000 shp); 2 propellers.
Sensors: 1 Hollandse DA 08 long-range air search radar; 1 Hollandse SGR 103 low-level air and sea search radar; 1 Hollandse SGR 105 sea search and navigational radar; 3 Hollandse M45 fire control radars; 1 Atlas hull-mounted sonar; naval tactical data system.
Armament: 4 Exocet anti-ship missile launchers; 3 single 100 mm dual-purpose guns; 4 twin Breda 40 mm anti-aircraft guns; 4 single heavyweight anti-submarine torpedo tubes; 2 quadruple-barrelled Bofors 375 mm anti-submarine rocket launchers; mines.
Top speed: 35 knots.   **Range:** 5,000 nautical miles at 18 knots.
Programme: Laid down between January 1959 and February 1961, this 4 ship class comprises *Hamburg* (D181), *Schleswig-Holstein* (D182), *Bayern* (D183) and *Hessen* (D184). The ships entered service in March 1964, October 1964, July 1965 and October 1968, respectively. All 4 destroyers underwent major modernisation between November 1974 and December 1976, during which Exocets replaced what had been the third, or 'X' positioned gun turret.
Notes: despite their inability to operate helicopters, these ships pack a considerable anti-ship punch out to about 22.7 nautical miles (42 kilometres).

Iroquois class

Destroyers

Canada's HMCS Huron *(DDH281), June 1984.*

Role: Anti-submarine.
Builders: Marine Industries and Davie, Canada.
User: Canadian Armed Forces, Marine Command.
Basic data: 4,200 tons full displacement; 425 ft (129.5 m) overall length; 50 ft (15.2 m) maximum beam.　　　　　**Crew:** 285.
Propulsion: 2 Pratt & Whitney FT4 gas turbines (total 50,000 shp) or 2 Pratt & Whitney FT12 gas turbines (total 7,400 shp); COGOG; 2 controllable-pitch propellers.
Sensors: 1 SPS-502 long-range air search radar; 1 SPQ-2D air and sea search radar; 2 Hollandse WM22 fire control radars; 3 sonars, comprising SQS-501 and SQS-505 hull-mounted and SQS-505 towed variable depth sonar; Litton automated action data processing.
Armament: 2 Sikorsky Sea King helicopters; 1 OTO-Melara 127 mm dual-purpose gun; 2 quadruple Sea Sparrow point air defence missile launchers; 1 Mk 10 Limbo anti-submarine mortar; 2 triple lightweight anti-submarine torpedo tubes.
Top speed: 29 knots.　　　　**Range:** 4,500 nautical miles at 20 knots.
Programme: A 4 ship class, the first two ships, HMCS *Iroquois* (DDH280) and HMCS *Huron* (DDH281), were both built by Marine Industries, being both laid down in January 1969. The other pair, HMCS *Athabascan* (DDH282) and HMCS *Algonquin* (DDH283), were laid down by Davie Shipbuilders in June and September 1969, respectively. The acceptance dates of all 4 ships were; July 1972, December 1972, November 1972 and September 1973.
Notes: The ship's 'boxy' superstructure sports V-shaped funnels: a configuration which, like so many other features of this class, including their large size relative to earlier Canadian frigates, was predicated by the need to operate two large helicopters in rough seas, day or night.

Georges Leygues class   Destroyers

Georges Leygues (*D640*), *showing the ship's generally low profile.*

Role: Anti-submarine.   **Builder:** DCAN Brest, France.
User: French Navy.
Basic data: 4,170 tons full displacement; 456 ft (139 m) overall length; 45.9 ft (14 m) maximum beam.   **Crew:** 216.
Propulsion: 2 Rolls-Royce TM3B Olympus turbines (total 56,000 shp) or 2 SEMT-Pielstick 16 PA 6 CV diesels (10,400 bhp); CODOG; 2 controllable-pitch propellers.
Sensors: 1 DRBV 51 long-range air search radar; 1 DRBV 26 low-level air search radar; 1 DRBC 32 fire control radar; 2 Decca 1226 sea search and navigational radars; 1 DUBV 23 hull-mounted sonar; 1 DUBV 43 variable depth sonar; SENIT 4 automated action information data processing system.
Armament: 2 Westland Lynx helicopters; 4 Exocet anti-ship missile launchers; 1 single 100 mm Model 1968 dual-purpose gun; 1 octuple Crotale point air defence missile launcher; 2 single 20 mm anti-aircraft guns; 2 heavyweight anti-submarine torpedo catapults.
Top speed: 30 knots.   **Range:** 9,500 nautical miles at 17 knots.
Programme: Currently a 7 ship class comprising : *Georges Leygues* (D640), *Dupleix* (D641), *Montcalm* (D642), *Jean de Vienne* (D643), *Primauget* (D644), *La Motte Piquet* (D645) and D646. Launched in December 1976, December 1978 and May 1983, respectively, the first 3 of this class entered service in December 1979, June 1981 and May 1982. *Jean de Vienne* entered service in 1983, with the 5th, 6th and 7th destroyers planned for delivery in 1986, 1987 and 1988. The first of two much modified anti-aircraft derivatives of this class, referred to as C70AAs, or Cassard class, and built by DCAN Lorient, was ordered in September 1981 and should enter service in 1988.
Notes: Very much contemporaries of the Royal Netherlands Navy's Kortenear class and Royal Navy's Broadsword class frigates, the

George Leygues class, or Type C 70 destroyers carry a potent-looking anti-submarine sensor/weapons fit, particularly for the more distant from ship type of subsurface operations. Further, the ability to carry a second helicopter is not only of material advantage to the ship's primary anti-submarine role, but could well prove valuable in the anti-shipping environment relating to both over-the-horizon missile targeting and for providing an additional airborne strike capability against hostile fast attack craft. The combination of the 100 mm dual-purpose gun and Crotale point air defence missile (26 rounds carried) provides the ship with a useful anti-air capability.

Georges Leygues (*D640*). *Note her Crotale missiles launcher atop the hangar.*

Luta class   Destroyers

Luta class 163 with its 2 sets of upward tilted and swivelling anti-ship missile launchers clearly visible, each being located immediately aft of the ship's raked twin funnels.

Role: General purpose.
Builders: Various, Chinese People's Republic.
User: Navy of the Chinese People's Republic.
Basic data: 3,960 tons full displacement; 418.3 ft (127.5 m) overall length; 42.3 ft (12.9 m) maximum beam.   **Crew:** Around 300.
Propulsion: 2 geared steam turbines (total 60,000 shp); 2 propellers.
Sensors: 1 long range air search radar; 1 short range combined air/sea search radar; 1 navigational radar; 2 separate types of fire control radars (not fitted to all ships); 1 or more hull-mounted sonars.
Armament: 2 triple SS-N-2 Styx-type anti-ship missile launchers; 2 twin 130 mm dual-purpose guns; 4 twin 57 mm or 37 mm anti-aircraft guns; 2 twin 25 mm anti-aircraft guns; 2 twelve-barrelled 250 mm anti-submarine rocket launchers; 2 depth charge racks; mines.
Top speed: 32 knots.   **Range:** 4,000 nautical miles at 15 knots.
Programme: Believed to be at least a 10 ship class, the lead ship was constructed at the Luta Shipyards in Kuangchou, with others known to have been built in another Shanghai shipyard. The first of class is reported to have entered service during 1972. One of this class is known to have exploded and sunk in August 1978. Known pennant numbers given to these ships include; *105, 106, 107, 131, 132, 160, 162* and *163.*
Notes: Although very similar in layout and general appearance to the Soviet Navy's Kotlin class destroyers, the Luta design is somewhat heavier, in part attributable to the installation of the two large triple-tubed anti-ship missile launchers which the Kotlins lack. While the Luta class pack a potentially potent anti-ship weapons punch, the effectiveness of this primary armament could well be diluted in a modern combat environment as a result of the seeming lack of current technology shipboard sensors.

Aconit type

Destroyers

Aconit (*D609*) *prior to installation of Exocet.*

Role: Anti-submarine. **Builder:** DCAN Lorient, France.
User: French Navy.
Basic data: 3,840 tons full displacement; 416.7 ft (127.0 m) overall
length; 44.0 ft (13.4 m) maximum beam. **Crew:** 232.
Propulsion: 1 Rateau double reduction geared steam turbine
(31,500 shp); 1 propeller.
Sensors: 1 DRBV 22A air search and height finder (3-D) radar; 1
DRBN 32 sea search and navigational radar; 1 DRBV 13 fire control
radar (Malafon); 1 DRBC 32B gun fire control radar; 1 DUBV 23
bow-mounted sonar; 1 DUBV 43 variable depth sonar; SENIT III
automated action information data processing system.
Armament: 1 Malafon anti-submarine missile launcher; 2 single
100 mm Model 1968 dual-purpose guns; 1 quadruple 305 mm anti-
submarine rocket mortar; 2 heavyweight anti-submarine torpedo catapults. Note; 4 MM 40 Exocets were being fitted during recent refit,
replacing the originally fitted 305 mm anti-submarine rocket mortar.
Top speed: 27 knots. **Range:** 5,000 nautical miles at 18 knots.
Programme: The sole *Aconit* (D609), or Type C 65 design, was laid
down in 1967 and entered service in March 1973.
Notes: All the evidence points to the *Aconit* being something of an
unfruitful excursion in meeting its operational design aims; the mission
requirement of which is now being met by the Georges Leygues class
destroyers. Unlike these later destroyers, *Aconit* carries no pad or facilities from which to operate anti-submarine helicopters, has little effective
anti-air capability from aft attack and seems potentially more vulnerable
to mechanical failure than most warships, thanks to its single propeller
shaft propulsion.

Hatsuyuki class   Destroyers

Japan's Hatsuyuki *(DDG122), lead of this 13 ship class. Note the tall mainmast, bulky funnel and aft superstructure.*

Role: General purpose.   **Builders:** Various, Japan.
User: Japanese Maritime Self-Defence Force.
Basic data: 3,700 tons full displacement; 432.1 ft (131.7 m) overall length; 44.9 ft (13.7 m) maximum beam.   **Crew:** 190.
Propulsion: 2 Kawasaki-built Rolls-Royce Olympus TM3B gas turbines (total 56,780 shp) or 2 Rolls-Royce Tyne RM1C gas turbines (total 10,680 shp); COGOG; 2 controllable-pitch propellers. Note: later ships will employ a Rolls-Royce Spey-Tyne COGAG arrangement similar to that fitted to Broadsword Batch II and III class Royal Navy frigates.
Sensors: 1 OPS-18 long range air search radar; 1 OPS-14B sea search and navigational radar; 1 FCS-2 (missile) and 1 GFCS-2 (gun) fire control radars; 1 OQS-4 hull-mounted sonar, automated action information data processing system.
Armament: 1 Kawasaki-built SH-3 Sea King helicopter; 2 quadruple Harpoon anti-ship missile launchers; 1 octuple Sea Sparrow point air defence missile launcher; 1 octuple ASROC anti-submarine missile launcher; 1 single 76 mm, OTO-Melara compact dual-purpose gun; 2 Phalanx 20 mm close-in weapons systems; 2 triple lightweight anti-submarine torpedo tubes.
Top speed: 30 knots. **Range:** Over 4,500 nautical miles at 18 knots.
Programme: At least a 13 ship class, of which 13 had been ordered on an incremental basis by the spring of 1984. The lead ship, *Hatsuyuki* (DDG122), was ordered in 1977, laid down in March 1979, launched in November 1980 and delivered in March 1983, following extended lead of class trials. *Shirayuki* (123), *Mireyuki* (124), *Sawuyuki* (125) and *Hamayuki* (126) had all been laid down between December 1979 and April 1982; these ships being launched between August

80

1981 and October 1982. A further 8 destroyers, *Isoyuki* (127), *Hara-yuki* (128), *Yamayuki* (129), *Matsuyuki* (130), plus 131 through 134, had been laid down by early 1985. Five shipyards are involved in the programme: Sumitomo as the lead yard, along with Hitachi, Mitsubishi, Ishikawajima Heavy Industries and Mitsui.

Notes: While the weapons fit of the Hatsuyuki class is still biased towards the anti-submarine warfare role, these destroyers carry a good secondary anti-ship and defensive anti-air armament capability, aspects that reflect both the quantitative and qualitative growth of the Soviet naval presence around the Japanese islands within the past 15 or more years. Of equal technical interest is the Japanese Maritime Self-Defence Force's selection of British rather than US propulsive machinery for these ships; a choice that ran counter to the previous Japanese naval preference either to buy or build adaptations of US systems and equipment. The construction of the Hatsuyuki class represents the largest single Japanese naval programme to be put underway since World War II and will add considerably to the stature of this already respectably-sized navy.

Hatsuyuki (*DDG122*), with Sea Sparrow launcher just visible aft of her helipad.

Gearing class   Destroyers

Toumbazis (*D215*) *serves with the Greek Navy.*

Role: Anti-submarine.   **Builders:** Various, USA.
Users: Navies of Argentine (1 ship), Brazil (2), Ecuador (1), Greece (7), Mexico (2), Pakistan (6), South Korea (7), Spain (5), Taiwan (14), and Turkey (9).
Basic data: 3,520 tons full displacement, 390.5 ft (119 m) overall length; 40.85 ft (12.45 m) maximum beam.   **Crew:** c. 275.
Propulsion: 2 geared steam turbines (total 60,000 shp); 2 propellers.
Sensors: 1 SPS-40 long-range air search radar; 1 SPS-10 sea search and navigational radar; 1 SQS-23 hull-mounted sonar.
Armament: The original weapons fit comprised: 3 twin 5 inch guns; 12 single 40 mm anti-aircraft guns; 10 heavyweight anti-submarine torpedo tubes (some ships had 16 anti-aircraft guns, no torpedoes). Most ships currently operate with only 2 twin 5 inch guns and 2 triple lightweight anti-submarine torpedo tubes. Argentine ships carry 2 twin Exocet anti-ship missile launchers, while South Korean ships carry 2 quadruple Harpoon anti-ship missile launchers; 1 octuple ASROC anti-submarine missile launcher is fitted to some ships of the Brazilian, Pakistani and Spanish navies. Most Argentinian, Greek and Spanish vessels have a helicopter pad immediately aft of the rear superstructure.
Top speed: 33 knots.   **Range:** 4,000 nautical miles at 20 knots.
Programme: A 98 ship class built between 1945 and 1952.
Notes: Essentially the Allen M. Sumner class design stretched by 14 feet (4.27 m) amidships. 48 remain in service.

Modified Kildin/Kildin class   Destroyers

The Modified Kildin class Soviet destroyer, Prozorlivyy.

Role: Anti-ship.   **Builders:** Various, USSR.
User: Soviet Navy.
Basic data: 3,500 tons full displacement; 413 ft (126 m) overall
length; 42.3 ft (12.9 m) maximum beam.   **Crew:** 300.
Propulsion: 2 geared steam turbines (total 72,000 shp); 2 propellers.
Sensors: 1 long-range air search radar; 1 sea search and navigational
radar; 3 fire control radars; 1 hull-mounted sonar.
Armament: 4 single SS-N-2C anti-ship missile launchers on Modified ships only (1 single SS-N-1 anti-ship cruise missile launcher on
sole Kildin); 2 twin 76 mm anti-aircraft guns on Modified ships only,
4 quadruple 57 mm anti-aircraft guns; 2 RB6000 twelve-barrel 250 mm
anti-submarine rocket launchers; 2 twin heavyweight anti-submarine
torpedo tubes.
Top speed: 34 knots.   **Range:** 4,000 nautical miles at 18 knots.
Programme: This 4 ship class completed at the close of the 1950s
comprises: *Bedovy, Neuderzhimyy, Prozorlivyy* and *Neulovimyy.* All
but the latter ship were converted to Modified Kildins between 1973
and 1975. It is doubtful if the remaining vessel, which serves with the
Soviet Pacific fleet, will be converted.
Notes: A development of the earlier Kotlin class anti-submarine destroyers, the Kildins represent an interim design solution to the anti-
carrier centred task group ship requirement, aimed at supplementing
the Kashin class destroyers already in service.

Almirante Brown class   Destroyers

Almirante Brown (*D10*) *and lead of class at speed.*

Role: General-purpose.
Builder: Blohm und Voss, Federal Germany. **User:** Argentinian Navy.
Basic data: 3,360 tons full displacement; 412.1 ft (126.6 m) overall
length; 43.1 ft (15.0 m) maximum beam.   **Crew:** 230.
Propulsion: 2 Rolls-Royce TM3B Olympus gas turbines (total
56,800 shp) or 2 Rolls-Royce Tyne RM1C gas turbines (total 10,800
shp); COGOG; 2 controllable-pitch propellers.
Sensors: 1 Hollandse DA 08A air search radar; 1 Decca 1226 sea
search and navigational radar; 1 each Hollandes STIR (for missiles) and
WM25 (for guns) fire control radars; 1 Hollandse LIROD optronic
fire control system; 1 Krupp Atlas 80 hull-mounted sonar; SATIR
automated action information data processing system.
Armament: 2 Lynx-sized helicopters; 8 MM 40 Exocet anti-ship missile launchers; 1 octuple Aspide point air defence missile launcher; 1
single 127 mm OTO-Melara compact dual-purpose gun; 4 twin 40 mm
Breda/Bofors close-in weapons systems; 2 triple lightweight anti-
submarine torpedo tubes.
Top speed: 30.5 knots.   **Range:** 4,500 nautical miles at 18 knots.
Programme: Ordered by the Argentinian Government in December
1978, the original contract was for 6 ships, 4 of which were to be built
in Argentina. However, by July 1979, the contract was ratified around
4 ships, all to be built by Blohm und Voss, while Argentina was to
build 6 of the smaller Blohm und Voss MEKO 140 corvettes in its own
shipyards. The 4 Argentinian destroyers are a variant of the basic
Blohm und Voss MEKO design and comprise: *Almirante Brown* (D10),
La Argentina (D11), *Heroina* (D12) and *Sarandi* (D13). All launched

between the close of March 1981 and the end of August 1982, *Almirante Brown* was accepted by the Argentinian Navy in February 1983, with the remaining 3 ships all having entered service by late 1984.

Notes: This class differs from the initial MEKO 360 design (see the Nigerian Navy's *Arudu* frigate) in that it employs an all gas turbine propulsive arrangement, supplied by Rolls-Royce and saving some 320 tons in terms of the ships' full displacement. In terms of sensors and weapons fit, these 4 destroyers add a new and formidable element to the Argentinian Navy's overall capability. Two other design aspects of these ships are of interest, namely, the MEKO building block system for the various weapons and electronics shipboard packages employed, along with the choice of construction materials used. In the case of the MEKO building block philosophy, which involves pre-packaging virtually everything from gun mountings to prime propulsive machinery, the system significantly reduces the amount of time that the ship has to spend in dock, non-operational. Turning to the materials employed within both hull and superstructure, it is interesting to note that the builders have elected to use steel throughout; a choice that cannot but enhance the ship's survivability in terms of tolerance to battle damage.

Almirante Brown (*D10*) and L'Argentina (*D11*) *sailing in company.*

Fletcher class   Destroyers

The Brazilian Navy's Piaui *(D31).*

Role: General purpose.   **Builders:** Various, USA.
Users: Navies of Brazil (3 ships), Greece (6), Mexico (1), South Korea
(2), Spain (5) and Taiwan (4).
Basic data: 2,850 tons full displacement; 376.8 ft (114.85 m) overall
length; 39.5 ft (12.0 m) maximum beam.   **Crew:** around 265.
Propulsion: 2 geared steam turbines (total 60,000 shp); 2 propellers.
Sensors: All ships carry 1 SPS-6 air search radar and 1 SPS-10 sea
search and navigational radar. All ships fitted with sonar, mainly
SQS-4 or -29. Various fire control radars equip the ships of Brazil,
Greece, Spain, Taiwan and Turkey.
Armament: Original fit comprised: 5 single 5 inch guns; 6 or 10 single
40 mm anti-aircraft guns; 10 heavyweight torpedo tubes and depth
charges. Some ships still carry the full primary gun complement, but
most now only carry 4. Similarly, only the navies of Brazil, South Korea
and Spain retain the 40 mm guns, the rest having switched to 6 single
76 mm guns. Anti-submarine torpedoes are still carried, but current
installations consist of either 5 heavyweight or 6 lightweight torpedo
tubes. All ships still mount a Hedgehog depth charge mortar.
Top speed: 32–36 knots.   **Range:** 5,000 nautical miles at 15 knots.
Programme: In all, 180 Fletcher class destroyers were built in
numerous US shipyards between 1942 and 1944.
Notes: Just 20 of these elderly ships still serve in mid-1985.

Minegumo class   Destroyers

Minegumo (*D116*) *of the Japanese Maritime Self-Defence Force.*

Role: Anti-submarine.   **Builders:** Various, Japan.
User: Japanese Maritime Self-Defence Force.
Basic data: 2,750 tons full displacement; 377 ft (114.9 m) overall length; 37.7 ft (11.8 m) maximum beam.   **Crew:** 215.
Propulsion: 6 Mitsubishi 12UEV 30/40 diesels (total 26,500 bhp); 2 propellers.
Sensors: 1 OPS 11 long-range air search radar; 1 OPS 17 surface search and navigational radar; 1 SPG-34 gun fire control radar; 1 OQS 3 hull-mounted sonar; 1 SQS-35 towed variable depth sonar on F118.
Armament: 2 twin 76 mm dual-purpose guns; 1 Bofors 375 mm anti-submarine rocket launcher; 2 triple lightweight anti-submarine torpedo tubes. Note: F118 carries 1 octuple Mk 16 launcher for ASROC anti-submarine missile aft and has had aft twin gun turret replaced by 1 single 76 mm OTO-Melara gun. All 3 ships will be fitted with ASROC and all 3 will end up with OTO-Melara guns.
Top speed: 27 knots.   **Range:** 7,000 nautical miles at 20 knots.
Programme: This 3 ship class comprises *Minegumo* (D116), *Natsugumo* (D117) and *Murakumo* (D118), built by Mitsui, Uraga and Maizuru, respectively. Laid down between March 1967 and October 1968, all 3 ships entered service between August 1968 and August 1970.
Notes: Finely proportioned, handsome ships, the Minegumo class are a development of the Yamagumo class vessels. The Minegumos may be most economic vessels to operate but appear generally underarmed.

Broadsword class Batch II and III   Frigates

This abeam view of HMS Beaver *(F93) emphasises the newly adopted highly raked 'clipper' bow.*

Role: Anti-submarine.
Builders: Yarrow and Swan Hunter, UK.   **User:** Royal Navy.
Basic data: 4,350 tons (early Batch II) to 4,700 tons (Batch III) full displacement; 479.25 ft (146.1 m) overall length; 48.5 ft (14.75 m) maximum beam.   **Crew:** 250 (Batch II); around 270 (Batch III).
Propulsion: 2 Rolls-Royce Olympus TM3B gas turbines (total 54,400 shp) or 2 Rolls-Royce Tyne RM1C gas turbines (total 10,680 shp); COGOG on F92, F93 and F95; others have 2 Rolls-Royce Spey Sm1A gas turbines (total 36,000 shp) and 2 Rolls-Royce Tyne RM1C gas turbines (total 10,680 shp); COGAG. All ships have 2 controllable-pitch propellers.
Sensors: 1 Type 968 air search radar; 1 Type 967 (back-to-back) sea search radar; 1 Type 1006 navigational radar; 2 Type 911 Sea Wolf fire control radars; 1 Type 2016 hull-mounted sonar; Ferranti CAAIS automated action information data processing system.
Armament: 2 Westland Lynx helicopters; 4 MM38 Exocet anti-ship missile launchers; 2 sextuple Sea Wolf point air defence missile launchers; 2 triple lightweight anti-submarine torpedo tubes; 2 single 40 mm Bofors anti-aircraft guns (to be supplemented by 2 multi-barrelled 30 mm Hollandse/General Electric Goalkeeper close-in weapons systems on all ships); 1 single 4.5 Mk 8 dual-purpose gun to be fitted to Batch III ships.
Top speed: 30 knots (early Batch II) or 28 knots (all others)
Range: 4,500 nautical miles at 18 knots.
Programme: Ordered between April 1979 and December 1982, the 6 ships of Batch II comprise: HMS *Boxer* (F92), HMS *Beaver* (F93), HMS *Brave* (F94), HMS *London* (F95), HMS *Sheffield* (F96) and HMS *Coventry* (F98); all but the latter 2 Swan Hunter-built ships,

being constructed by Yarrow, the lead yard. The initial order for 2 of the reported planned 4 Batch III procurement was placed with Yarrow in December 1982, followed by 2 further ships in January 1985. The Batch III vessels so far identified are the lead, HMS *Cornwall* (F99), HMS *Cumberland* (F85), HMS *Campbeltown* (F86) and HMS *Chatham* (F87); the latter two being built by Cammell Laird and Swan Hunter respectively.

Notes: With the design of the Batch II finalised long before the Falklands war could be foreseen, the new elongated hull and combined gas and gas (COGAG) propulsion arrangement promise to give these later Broadsword ships more fuel space, more fuel economy and, hence, more actual autonomy through reducing their reliance on frequent refuelling. The Batch III ships clearly reflect some of the Falklands war lessons in terms of weapons fit.

A model of HMS Cornwall *(F99) the first of the gun-equipped Broadsword Batch III frigate with EH-101 helicopter aft.*

Tromp class   Frigates

HNLMS Tromp *(F801) in a long, rolling sea.*

Role: General-purpose.   **Builder:** De Schelde, Netherlands.
User: Royal Netherlands Navy.
Basic data: 4,308 tons full displacement; 452.75 ft (138 m) overall
length; 48.9 ft (14.9 m) maximum beam.   **Crew:** 306.
Propulsion: 2 Rolls-Royce TM3B Olympus gas turbines (derated to
total 44,000 shp) or 2 Rolls-Royce Tyne RM1C gas turbine (total
8,200 shp); COGOG; 2 controllable-pitch propellers.
Sensors: 1 Hollandse SPS-01 long-range (3-D) air search radar; 1
Hollandse ZW05 sea search and navigational radar; 1 Hollandse WM25
fire control radar; 2 Hollandse SPG-51C fire control radar; 1 Hollandse
CWE 610 hull-mounted sonar; Hollandse SEWACO automated data
processing system.
Armament: 1 Westland Lynx helicopter; 2 quadruple Harpoon anti-
ship missile launchers; 1 Standard area air defence launcher system
with 40 missiles; 1 octuple Sea Sparrow short-range air defence missile
launcher; 1 twin 120 mm Bofors dual-purpose gun; 2 triple anti-
submarine lightweight torpedo tubes.
Top speed: 28 knots.   **Range:** 5,000 nautical miles at 18 knots.
Programme: This 2 ship class comprises HNLMS *Tromp* (F801) and
HNLMS *De Ruyter* (F806), laid down in August and December 1971,
respectively, *Tromp* was launched in June 1973 and entered service
in October 1975, while *De Ruyter* was launched in March 1974 and
joined the fleet in June 1976.
Notes: These two large frigates exemplify the enormous strides
made in shipborne armaments brought about by the introduction of
the guided missile, illustrated by the fact that these ships pack
considerably more firepower with greater strike range than that
carried aboard the two nearly 12,000 ton cruisers that they replaced.
Characterised by the massive bulbous radome that covers the ship's

powerful 3-D surveillance radar, the two Tromp class frigates serve as the flagships of the Royal Netherlands Navy, being used as the respective leaders of the two Netherlands Navy long-range, deep water task groups. Comparable in size to the Royal Navy's Sheffield class destroyers and the Broadsword class frigates, the Tromps carry a more balanced armament than either of their British counterparts, particularly in terms of the Tromp's two tier surface-to-air missile defences and the retention of twin dual-purpose guns as a back up to both the air defence and anti-ship missiles. In terms of weapons fit, itself a function of the ship's envisaged primary role, the Tromp's armament mix seems to follow that of the Soviet's Kashin class destroyer that first appeared in 1962, as does that of Italy's Audace class destroyer, a near contemporary of the Tromp frigates.

HNLMS De Ruyter (*F806*) *showing her V-shaped funnels and enclosed primary radar housing.*

Halifax class   Frigates

An impression of HMCS Halifax *(FFH330) as she will be.*

Role: Anti-submarine.
Builders: St John Shipbuilding and Marine Industries, Canada.
User: Canadian Navy.
Basic data: 4,200 tons full displacement; 488.0 ft (133.5 m) overall length; 53.8 ft (16.4 m) maximum beam.   **Crew:** 250.
Propulsion: 2 General Electric LM2500 gas turbines (total 50,000 shp); 1 Pielstick diesel (8,800 bhp); CODOG; 2 propellers.
Sensors: 1 SPS-49 long range air search radar; 1 LM Ericsson Sea Giraffe low-level air/sea search radar; 1 sea search and navigational radar; 2 Raytheon fire control radars for Sea Sparrow; 1 hull-mounted and 1 towed array sonar systems; automated action information data processing systems.
Armament: 1 Sikorsky Sea King helicopter; 2 quadruple Harpoon anti-ship missile launchers; 2 octuple silos for vertically launched Sea Sparrows point air defence missiles; 1 single 57 mm Bofors SAK Mk 2 dual-purpose gun; 1 Mk15 Phalanx 20 mm close-in weapons system; 2 triple 324 mm torpedo tubes.
Top speed: 28 knots.   **Range:** 4,500 nautical miles at 18 knots.
Programme: Authorised in December 1977, the lead ship contract for this 6 frigate class was awarded to St John Shipbuilding in June 1983. St John will build three, the others coming from Marine Industries comprising: HMCS *Halifax* (FFH330), HMCS *Vancouver* (FFH331), HMCS *Ville de Quebec* (FFH332), HMCS *Toronto* (FFH333), HMCS *Regina* (FFH334) and HMCS *Calgary* (FFH335). The lead ship *Halifax* should enter service in February 1989, with the final vessel in service by March 1992.
Notes: The Halifax class employ a steel hull and alloy superstructure.

Baleares class   Frigates

Baleares (*F71*) *with Standard area air defence missile launcher aft.*

Role: Area air defence.   **Builder:** Bazan, Spain.
User: Spanish Navy.
Basic data: 4,177 tons full displacement; 438.0 ft (133.8 m) overall length; 46.75 ft (14.25 m) maximum beam.   **Crew:** 256.
Propulsion: 1 Westinghouse geared steam turbine (35,000 shp); 1 propeller.
Sensors: 1 SPS-52A long-range air search and height finder (3-D) radar; 1 SPS-10 sea search radar; 1 Decca TM1226 sea search and navigational radar; 1 SPG-51C and 1 SPG-53B fire control radars for Standard missiles; 1 SQS-23 hull-mounted sonar; 1 SQS-35 variable depth sonar; NTDS automated action information data processing system.
Armament: 1 single Mk 22 launcher for 16 Standard area air defence missiles; 1 single 5-inch Mk 42 dual-purpose gun; 1 octuple ASROC anti-submarine missile launcher; 2 middle-weight anti-submarine torpedo tubes; 1 quadruple lightweight anti-submarine torpedo tube.
Top speed: 27 knots.   **Range:** 4,500 nautical miles at 20 knots.
Programme: This 5-ship class comprises; *Baleares* (F71), *Andalucia* (F72), *Cataluña* (F73), *Asturias* (F74) and *Extremadura* (F75). All entered service between September 1973 and November 1976.
Notes: A Spanish-built variant of the US Navy's Knox class frigates, the Baleares class trades off the facilities to operate a shipboard helicopter against the installation of the Standard area air defence missile launcher. The Baleares class ships are being retrofitted with the Spanish-developed 20 mm Meroka close-in weapons system and are scheduled to have Harpoon anti-ship missiles added during the early-to-mid-1980s.

Krivak I/II/III classes   Frigates

The Soviet's Krivak I Druzhnyy, *April 1984.*

Role: Anti-submarine.   **Builders:** Various, USSR.
Users: Soviet Navy and Soviet Marine Border Guard.
Basic data: 3,800 tons full displacement; 405 ft (123.5 m) overall length, ; 47 ft (14.3 m) maximum beam.   **Crew:** 185 to 200.
Propulsion: 2 gas turbines for boost (total 46,600 shp) or 2 gas turbines for cruise (total 24,200 shp); COGOG; 2 propellers.
Sensors: 1 long air search radar; 1 sea search and navigational radar; 4 (Krivak I, II) or 1 (Krivak III) missile fire control radars; 1 (Krivak I, II) or 2 (Krivak III) gun fire control radars; 1 hull-mounted and 1 variable depth sonars; automated action information data processing.
Armament: 1 Kamov Ka 25 or 27 helicopter (Krivak III only); 1 quadruple SS-N-14 anti-submarine missile launcher; 2 twin (Krivak I, II) or 1 twin (Krivak III) short range anti-air missile launchers; 2 single (Krivak II) or 1 single (Krivak III) 100 mm or 2 twin (Krivak I) 76 mm dual-purpose guns; 2 multi-barrelled 30 mm close-in weapons (Krivak III only); 2 twelve-barrel 250 mm RBU 6000 anti-submarine rocket launchers; 2 quadruple 533 mm torpedo tubes (Krivak I, II only).
Top speed: 32 knots.
Range: 700 nautical miles at 30 knots/4,000 nautical miles at 19 knots.
Programme: Construction of the initial Krivak Is commenced around late 1967 with the lead ship going to sea in 1970. Since then, at least, five separate Soviet shipyards have been involved in building the 21 Krivak Is, 11 Krivak IIs and 1 Krivak III known to have been completed by early 1985, when work on a further 2 Krivak IIIs was underway. While the first of the Krivak IIs, delivered in 1976, differed relatively slightly from the Krivak I, with changes being confined largely to fitting a set of larger calibre gun turrets and improved variable depth sonar, the lead Krivak III, delivered during 1984, represents a major redesign

involving the deletion of most of the ship's earlier armament for the new helicopter operating capability.

Notes: The Krivak I and II classes are contemporaries of the Kresta II class cruisers and, as such, must be seen as part of the Soviet Navy's broader evolution of thinking concerning their operational tasks and the fleet composition required to meet these requirements. The emergence of the Krivaks and Kresta IIs, both of which were dedicated submarine killers, showed that the Soviet Navy was no longer concerned solely with questions of countering the threats posed by a carrier-centred task group, but were now addressing the anti-submarine problem much more directly. As with other recent Soviet warships the Krivak Is and IIs certainly pack the maximum amount of weaponry into a ship of their size, the primary element of which is the four per ship SS-N-14 'Silex' anti-submarine missiles, reported to cruise at around 645 mph out to a maximum effective range of 30 nautical miles. Backing up this primary armament, each of the Krivak I and II frigates is equipped with the longer ranging 21 inch (533 mm) heavyweight torpedo, as opposed to the lighter 12.8 inch (324 mm) torpedoes carried by the Krivak I and II's Western contemporaries. On first sight, the Krivak III appears to offer a somewhat questionable weapons trade-off in order to carry one hangared helicopter. However, it is of interest to note that the lead Krivak III was actually delivered to the Soviet Marine Border Guard, an arm of the KGB and not the Soviet Navy, and therefore may have been designed to meet mission needs quite different from those of the earlier frigates.

Menzhinsky, *first of the helicopter-equipped Krivak IIIs.*

Bremen class   Frigates

Bremen (*F207*) *on initial sea trials, May 1981.*

Role: General-purpose.   **Builders:** Various, Federal Germany.
User: Federal German Navy.
Basic data: 3,800 tons full displacement; 426.5 ft (130 m) overall
length; 47.25 ft (14.4 m) maximum beam.   **Crew:** 200.
Propulsion: 2 General Electric LM2500 gas turbines (total
50,000 shp) or 2 MTU Type 20V 956 TB 92 diesels (total
10,400 bhp); CODOG; 2 controllable-pitch propellers.
Sensors: 1 Hollandse DA 08 air and sea search radar; 1 SMA 3 RM
20 sea search and navigational radar; 1 Hollandse WM25 and 1 Hollandse STIR fire control radars; 1 Krupp Atlas DSQS-21BZ hull-
mounted sonar; SATIR automated action information data processing.
Armament: 2 Westland Lynx helicopters; 2 quadruple Harpoon
long-range anti-ship missile launchers; 1 OTO-Melara 76 mm dual-
purpose gun; 1 octuple Sea Sparrow point air defence missile launcher;
2 twin lightweight anti-submarine torpedo tubes; provision for twin
24-cell RAM close-in air defence missile launchers.
Top speed: 30 knots.   **Range:** 4,000 nautical miles at 18 knots.
Programme: The first 6 of what was to be a 12 ship class were
ordered in July 1977. The 9th through 12th ships were cancelled in
mid-1980, while the fate of the 7th and 8th vessels remains uncertain,
the 6 frigates currently being operated are *Bremen* (F207), *Nieder-
sachsen* (F208), *Rheinland-Pfalz* (F209), *Emden* (F210), *Koln* (F211)
and *Karlsruhe* (F212). The construction programme has been spread
widely around the West German naval shipbuilders, with Bremer Vulkan acting as lead yard and responsible for the building of F207 and
sensor/weapon system fitment to all vessels. Blohm und Voss, the large
Hamburg-based yard, built F209 and F211, while AG Weser built F208
and Thyssen Nordseewerke built F210 and Howaldtswerke-Deutsche
Werft built F212. All 6 frigates were launched between September

1979 and January 1982, and all entered service between May 1982 and April 1984.

Notes: Conceived as replacement for the existing Type 120 or Koln class frigates; the Type 122 or Bremen class design is based on the Dutch-developed Standard or Kortenaer class hull, but breaks with the Dutch design in adopting a combined diesel or gas turbine machinery solution. While the primary anti-ship and air defence missile complement of the Dutch and West German ships is the same, the Bremens carry only 1 OTO-Melara 76 mm gun, deleting the Dutch vessel's aft-mounted 76 mm for space provision in which to fit the General Dynamics-developed RAM rapid response, close-in air defence missile system. The Bremen class frigates DA 08 medium-range radar is quoted as being able to detect an incoming combat aircraft at around 45 nautical miles, while the Sea Sparrow missiles are effective out to around 8 nautical miles and altitudes up to around 20,000 feet.

Rheinland-Pfalz (*F209*) *operating with a Type 206 submarine.*

Kortenaer class   Frigates

HNLMS Banckert (*F810*) *1981*.

Role: Anti-submarine.
Builders: De Schelde and Wilton-Fijenoord (F823, F824 only), Netherlands.
Users: Royal Netherlands Navy, Hellenic (Greek) Navy.
Basic data: 3,750 tons full displacement; 420 ft (1.28 m) overall length; 47.3 ft (14.4 m) maximum beam.   **Crew:** 200.
Propulsion: 2 Rolls-Royce TM3B Olympus gas turbines (total 56,800 shp) or 2 Rolls Royce Tyne RM1C gas turbines (total 10,800 shp); COGOG; 2 controllable-pitch propellers.
Sensors: 1 Hollandse LW08 long-range 3-D air search radar; 1 Hollandse DA 05 sea search and navigational radar; 1 Hollandse M45 fire control radar (76 mm gun); 1 Hollandse fire control radar (Sea Sparrow); 1 Hollandse SQS 505 hull-mounted sonar; Hollandse SEWACO automated action information data processor.
Armament: 2 Westland Lynx helicopters; 2 quadruple Harpoon anti-ship missile launchers; 1 octuple Sea Sparrow close-in air defence missile launcher; 1 single 76 mm OTO-Melara dual-purpose guns; 1 single 40 mm anti-aircraft gun; 2 twin lightweight anti-submarine torpedo tubes. F812 and F813 have 1 single Mk 13 launcher for Standard area air defence missiles in place of helicopter hangar. Note that the second 76 mm gun originally fitted above the hangar has been replaced by a lighter 40 mm weapon.
Top speed: 30 knots.   **Range:** 4,700 nautical miles at 16 knots.
Programme: Currently a 14 ship class, the original 12 Dutch vessels were ordered in 3 batches (4 each) between August 1974 and December 1976, the first keel being laid in April 1975. In September 1980, Greece placed an order for 1 of this class and took options to buy 2

more (1 to be built in Greece). The Greek need for early delivery led the Dutch to reallocate what should have been their 6th ship to Greece and the same procedure was followed with the planned 7th Dutch vessel, when Greece took up its first option in July 1981. The Dutch ships, along with the year of their completion, are: *Kortenaer* (F807) 1978, *Callenburgh* (F808) 1979, *Van Kinsbergen* (F809) 1980, *Banckert* (F810) 1980, *Piet Heyn* (F811) 1981, *Abraham Crijnssen* (F816) 1982, *Philips van Almonde* (F823) 1981, *Bloys van Treslong* (F824) 1982, *Jan van Brakel* (F825) 1982 and *Pieter Florisz* (F826) 1983. The 2 modified ships, *Jacob van Heemskerck* (F812) 1985 and *Witte de With* (F813) 1986, are referred to as Van Heemskerck class frigates. The 2 Greek vessels are *Elli* (F450) 1981 and *Lemnos* (F451) 1982.

Notes: Initially referred to as Standard or S frigates (relating to the Standard NATO Frigate concept around which they were designed), the Kortenaer class display functional, relatively compact lines. In functional terms, the Kortenaers' primary role is the same as that of the Royal Navy's Broadswords, US Navy's Perry class and French Navy's Georges Leygues vessels. While of the four rival designs, the French vessel would appear to carry the most comprehensive anti-submarine package of sensors and weapons, the Kortenaers embody the most balanced sensor/weapons fit in terms of offensive and defensive armament. Under a collaborative agreement signed in 1975 between the West German and Dutch Governments, the hull and much of the Kortenaer's internal design layout has been adopted as the basis for West Germany's Type 122 Bremen class frigate.

HNLMS Piet Heyn (*F811*) *with aft 76 mm gun replaced by 40 mm mount.*

Duke (Type 23) class   Frigates

A Yarrow model of the Royal Navy's latest Type 23 frigate as completed. Note the forward deck silo for the ship's 32 vertically launched Sea Wolf point air defence missiles.

Role: Anti-submarine.   **Builder:** Yarrow (lead yard), UK.
User: Under development for the Royal Navy.
Basic data: 3,700 tons full displacement; 436,4 ft (133.0 m) overall length; 51.8 ft (15.8 m) maximum beam.   **Crew:** 177.
Propulsion: 2 Rolls-Royce Spey SM1A gas turbines (total 36,000 shp) or/and 4 Paxman Valenta diesel generators (total 12,700 bhp) used to drive 2 electric propulsion motors; CODLAG; 2 propellers.
Sensors: 1 undesignated combined low level air/sea search and navigational radar; 2 Type 911 Sea Wolf fire control radars; 1 optronic fire control system; 1 Type 2050 hull-mounted and 1 towed array sonar; Ferranti automated action information data processing system.
Armament: 1 Sea King or EH-101 sized anti-submarine helicopter; 2 quadruple Exocet-sized anti-ship missile launchers; silo for 32 vertically launched Sea Wolf point air defence missiles; 1 single 4.5 inch Vickers Mk 8 dual-purpose gun; 2 single 30 mm Oerlikon anti-aircraft guns; 4 fixed tubes for lightweight anti-submarine torpedoes.
Top speed: Around 28 knots.
Endurance: Over 7,000 nautical miles.
Programme: As lead yard for the projected Royal Navy Type 23 frigate, Yarrow received their first design contract for this vessel during the latter half of 1982 followed by a contract, that to proceed with the construction of the lead ship, HMS *Norfolk* (F230) in October 1984. Contracts for the building of a 2nd and 3rd of class were being negotiated during the spring of 1985. The Duke class should form

the backbone of the Royal Navy's anti-submarine surface force by the year 2000, following delivery of the lead vessel during 1989.

Notes: Marginally longer and broader than a Batch 1 Broadsword class frigate, the Type 23 design incorporates a number of innovations for a British warship in terms of both weapons fit and propulsive machinery arrangement. In the context of weaponry, the Type 23 will be the first Royal Navy operational ship to deploy the vertically launched Sea Wolf system; an advance that promises to both extend the range of this highly agile point air defence missile and permit more missiles to be instantly available for launch in the case of a saturation attack from multiple threats. Turning to the novel-for-frigate propulsive machinery arrangement, the Type 23's system has been described as COmbined Diesel eLectric And Gas, or CODLAG; a combination that is claimed will enhance the performance of the ship's anti-submarine sensors by reducing ship's machinery-generated noise levels fairly significantly. Another aspect of more than passing interest to naval manpower planners is the Type 23's much reduced crew complement: more than a third down on that required to man a Batch II Broadsword; a factor that reflects very favourably in the context of overall ship operating costs. The unit cost of £110 million is quoted for the Type 23 frigate in 1984/5 values, exclusive of development costs. These ships are sometimes referred to as the Duke class, as each vessel will be named after famous noblemen, such as the Duke of Norfolk.

An abeam view of HMS Norfolk (F230) as she will appear.

Oliver Hazard Perry class   Frigates

USS Perry (*FFG7*) *on sea trials.*

Role: General-purpose.
Builders: Bath Iron Works & Todd Shipyards, USA; Bazan, Spain, and Williamstown Dockyards, Australia.
Users: Navies of the USA, Australia and Spain.
Basic data: 3,700 tons full displacement; 445 ft (135.6 m) overall length; 45 ft (13.7 m) maximum beam.   **Crew:** 180.
Propulsion: 2 General Electric LM2500 gas turbines (total 40,000 shp); COGAG; 1 controllable-pitch propeller.
Sensors: 1 SPS-49 long-range air search radar; 1 SPS-55 sea search and navigational search radar; 1 SPG-60 STIR fire control radar (missile); 1 Mk 92 fire control radar (gun); 1 SQS-56 hull-mounted sonar; NTDS automated action information data processing.
Armament: 2 up to Sikorsky SH-60 Seahawk sized helicopters; 1 single Mk 13 launcher for either Standard MR area air defence missiles or Harpoon anti-ship missiles; 1 single 76 mm Mk 75 anti-aircraft gun; 1 Phalanx 20 mm close-in weapons system; 2 triple lightweight anti-submarine torpedo tubes.
Top speed: 28 knots.   **Range:** 4,000 nautical miles at 20 knots.
Programme: A 50 ship US Navy class, plus 9 for overseas users, the lead of class, built by Bath Iron Works, was ordered in October 1973. The US Navy ships are: *Oliver Hazard Perry* (FFG7), *McInerney* (8), *Wadsworth* (9), *Duncan* (10), *Clark* (11), *George Philip* (12), *Samuel E. Morison* (13), *John H. Sides* (14), *Estocin* (15), *Clifton Sprague* (16), *John A. Moore* (19), *Antrim* (20), *Flatley* (21), *Fahrion* (22), *Lewis B. Puller* (23), *Jack Williams* (24), *Copeland* (25), *Gallery* (26), *Mahlon S. Tisdale* (27), *Boone* (28), *Stephen W. Groves* (29), *Reid* (30), *Stark* (31), *John L. Hall* (32), *Jarrett* (33), *Aubrey Fitch* (34), *Underwood* (36), *Crommelin* (37), *Curts* (38), *Doyle* (39), *Halyburton* (40), *McCluskey* (41), *Klakring* (42), *Thach* (43), *De Wert* (45), *Rentz*

(46), *Nicholas* (47), *Vandergrift* (48), *Robert G. Bradley* (49), *Gary* (51), *Carr* (52), *Hawes* (53), *Ford* (54), *Elrod* (55), *Simpson* (56), *Reuben James* (57), *Samuel B. Roberts* (58), *Kauffman* (59), *Rodney M. Davis* (60), and the as yet unnamed 61. *Perry* entered service in December 1977 and by July 1985 all but the last 6 US frigates were operational. Australia operates 4 as HMAS *Adelaide* (FFG01), *Canberra* (02), *Sydney* (03) and *Darwin* (04), all commissioned between November 1980 and July 1984. FFG05 and 06, to be built locally, were ordered in November 1983. Three Spanish ships, *Santa Maria* (FFG81), *Numancia* (82) and *Leon* (83), were in build or fitting out by mid-1985.

Notes: Unlovely-looking ships, the Perry class were designed for modular assembly to facilitate high-rate series production. In operational terms, the Perry class has been produced to provide oceangoing escort for merchantmen or a naval amphibious task force. As a result of the potential combat damage vulnerability of the single shaft/propeller arrangement adopted for the ship (itself an economy measure allowing the use of a standard Spruance class propulsion cell to be employed), the Perry class frigates are equipped with two diesel-driven retractable thrusters that can propel the ship through the water at up to 5 knots, should the main propulsion be lost. The position of the 76 mm OTO-Melara gun, between mast and funnel, significantly limits its arcs of fire.

Another view of Perry, *showing the ship's armament disposition*.

Aradu type

Frigates

NNS Aradu (*F89*), *flagship of the Nigerian Navy.*

Role: General purpose.
Builder: Blohm und Voss, Federal Germany.   **User:** Nigerian Navy.
Basic data: 3,680 tons full displacement; 412.1 ft (125.6 m) overall length; 43.1 ft (15.0 m) maximum beam.   **Crew:** 230.
Propulsion: 2 Rolls-Royce TM3B Olympus gas turbines (56,800 shp) or 2 MTU 20V956 TB92 diesels (total 11,070 bhp); CODOG; 2 controllable-pitch propellers.
Sensors: 1 Plessey AWS 5D long range air search and height finder (3-D) radar; 1 Decca TM1226 sea search and navigational radar; 1 Hollandse WM 25 fire control radar and automated action information data processing system: 1 Hollandse STIR fire control radar (missiles); 1 Hollandse PHS 32 hull-mounted sonar.
Armament: 1 Lynx helicopter; 8 MM 40 Exocet anti-ship missile launchers; 1 octuple Albatros (Sea Sparrow) point air defence missile launcher; 1 single 127 mm OTO-Melara dual-purpose gun; 4 twin 40 mm Breda/Bofors L70/40 anti-aircraft guns; 2 triple lightweight anti-submarine torpedo tubes.
Top speed: 29 knots.   **Range:** 4,500 nautical miles at 18 knots.
Programme: The sole Nigerian ship, NNS *Aradu* (F89), was ordered in November 1977 and entered service in July 1981.
Notes: NNS *Aradu* is a MEKO 360H-1 design, signifying that it carries only one helicopter, unlike the subsequent Argentinian Almirante Brown class MEKO 360H-2 destroyers that carry two each. The Nigerian ship also differs from the later Argentinian vessels in employing a gas turbine/diesel propulsion arrangement, as opposed to the all gas turbine system adopted by the Argentinian Navy.

Amazon class

Frigates

HMS Avenger *(F185) on sea trials, 1978.*

Role: General purpose. **Builders:** Various, UK.
User: Royal Navy.
Basic data: 3,250 tons full displacement; 385 ft (117.0 m) overall length; 41.75 ft (12.7 m) maximum beam. **Crew:** 171.
Propulsion: 2 Rolls-Royce TM3B Olympus gas turbines (total 56,000 shp) or 2 Rolls-Royce Tyne RMIA gas turbines (total 8,000 shp); COGOG; 2 controllable-pitch propellers.
Sensors: 1 Type 992Q air search radar; 1 Decca Type 978 sea search and navigational radar; 2 Selenia Orion missile/gun fire control radars; 4 hull-mounted sonars (Types 162M, 170B, 174 and 184).
Armament: A Westland Lynx helicopter; 4 Exocet anti-ship missile launchers; 1 Vickers 4.5 in Mk 8 gun; 1 quadruple Seacat surface-to-air missile launcher; 2 Oerlikon 20 mm guns; 2 triple anti-submarine lightweight-torpedo tubes.
Top speed: 32 knots. **Range:** 4,300 nautical miles at 17 knots.
Programme: All 8 of these Type 21 frigates were ordered within a 20 month period commencing late March 1969, the first 3 being built by Vosper Thornycroft, the lead yard, while the last 5 came from Yarrow. The ships and their commissioning dates are: HMS *Amazon* (F169), May 1974; HMS *Antelope* (F170), July 1975; HMS *Active* (F171), June 1977; HMS *Ambuscade* (F172), September 1975; HMS *Arrow* (F173), July 1976; HMS *Alacrity* (F174), July 1977; HMS *Ardent* (F184), October 1977; and HMS *Avenger* (F185), May 1978; F170 and F184 being lost in action during May 1982.
Notes: Sleek, fast and agile, the Type 21 were the first Royal Navy warships to be designed around all gas turbine propulsion from the outset.

USS Richard L. Page *(FFG5), part of the US Atlantic Fleet.*

Role: Anti-submarine.
User: US Navy.
Builders: Various, USA.
Basic data: 3,245 tons full displacement; 414.5 ft (126.3 m) overall length; 44.2 ft (13.5 m) maximum beam. **Crew:** 255.
Propulsion: 1 geared steam turbine (35,000 shp); 1 propeller.
Sensors: 1 SPS-52D combined air search and height finder (3-D) radar; 1 SPS-10F sea search and navigational radar; 1 SPG-51C missile fire control radar; 1 Mk 35 gun fire control radar; 1 SQS-26AX bow-mounted sonar; NTDS automated action information data processing system.
Armament: 1 Kaman SH-2 Seasprite helicopter; 1 single Mk 22 Tartar/Standard MR area air defence missile launcher; 1 single 5 inch Mk 30 dual-purpose gun; 1 octuple Mk 16 ASROC anti-submarine missile launcher; 2 triple lightweight anti-submarine torpedo tubes.
Top speed: 27 knots.   **Range:** 4,000 nautical miles at 20 knots.
Programme: Ordered in 2 batches of 3 ships during the 1962/3 period, this 6 ship class comprises: USS *Brooke* (FFG1), USS *Ramsey* (LFFG2), USS *Schofield* (FFG3), USS *Talbot* (FFG4), USS *Richard L. Page* (FFG5) and USS *Julius A. Furer* (FFG6). Lockheed Shipbuilding built the first 3 ships, with Bath Iron Works responsible for the others. Built between December 1962 and November 1967, all ships entered service between March 1966 and November 1967.
Notes: Employing the same hull design and layout as that of the Garcia class, the Brookes differ only in replacing the aft 5 inch gun with the Tartar/Standard missile launcher.

De Zeven Provincien class　　　　　　　　　　Frigates

An artist's impression of this new, rugged Dutch frigate.

Role: General purpose.　　　　　　**Builder:** De Schelde, Netherlands.
User: Royal Netherlands Navy.
Basic data: 3,200 tons full displacement; 374.3 ft (114.1 m) overall
length; 47.2 ft (14.4 m) maximum beam.　　　　　　**Crew:** 137.
Propulsion: 2 Rolls-Royce Spey SMIA (total 36,640 shp) or 2
SEMT-Pielstick diesels (total 8,500 bhp); CODOG; 2 controllable-
pitch propellers.
Sensors: 1 Hollandse DA 08 long range air search radar; 1 Hollandse
ZW 06 sea search and navigational radar; 1 Hollandse WM 25 fire con-
trol radar and optronics system; 1 PHS 36 bow-mounted and variable
depth sonar system; SEWACO automated action information data processing system.
Armament: 1 Westland Lynx helicopter; 2 quadruple Harpoon anti-
ship missile launchers; 1 octuple Sea Sparrow point air defence missile
launcher; 1 single 57 mm Bofors SAK 57 Mk 2 dual-purpose gun; 1
Hollandse/GE Goalkeeper 30 mm close-in weapons system; 2 twin
324 mm torpedo tubes.
Top speed: 30 knots.　　　　**Range:** 5,000 nautical miles at 18 knots.
Programme: An 8 ship class, the lead *De Zeven Provincien* (F827),
plus 3 more were ordered in June 1984, followed by the remaining 4
in June 1985. The lead ship should complete trials and commission
in 1988.
Notes: A well-armed, seaworthy-looking design, these M class-
frigates, as they were originally known, have emerged as somewhat
larger ships over the 6 or so years taken to finalise their detailed construction.

Maestrale class   Frigates

Libeccio (*F572*). *Note portside Otomat missile launchers atop helicopter hangar.*

Role: Anti-submarine.   **Builder:** CNR, Italy.
User: Italian Navy.
Basic data: 3.040 tons full displacement; 402,65 ft (122.73 m) overall length; 42.25 ft (12.88 m) maximum beam.   **Crew:** 232.
Propulsion: 2 General Electric LM 2500 gas turbines (total 50,000 shp) or 2 GMT B230-20DVM diesels (total 14,160 bhp); CODOG; 2 controllable-pitch propellers.
Sensors: 1 Selenia RAN 10S primary air/sea search radar; 1 SMA MM/SPS-702 close-in air/sea search radar; 1 SMA 3RM20 navigational radar; 1 ELSAG NA-30 fire control radar (guns); 2 Selenia RTN-30X fire control radars (missiles); 1 Raytheon DE 1164 integrated hull and variable depth sonars; Selenia IPN-10 automated action information data processing.
Armament: 2 Agusta-Bell 212 helicopters; 4 Otomat Mk 2 anti-ship missile launchers; 1 OTO-Melara 127 mm gun; 1 octuple Aspide medium-range air defence missile launcher; 2 Breda/Bofors 40 mm anti-aircraft guns; 2 each heavyweight and lightweight anti-submarine torpedo tubes.
Top speed: 33 knots.   **Range:** 6,000 nautical miles at 15 knots.
Programme: Subject of a special piece of Italian Government legislation passed in 1975 approving the construction of 8 Maestrale class frigates, 2 ships were deleted from the planned programme in 1977, but restored in October 1980. The class comprises: *Maestrale* (F570), *Grecale* (F571), *Libeccio* (F572), *Scirocco* (F573), *Aliseo* (F574), *Euro* (F575), *Espero* (F576) and *Zeffiro* (F577). The first of class, *Maestrale* (F570), was laid down in March 1978, launched in February 1981 and commissioned in March 1982. The 2nd through 5th vessels commissioned during 1983 and all were in service by 1985.

Notes: Although exhibiting a strong family resemblance to the smaller Lupo class frigates that came from the same drawing boards, the Maestrale class is, in mission terms, more readily related to the Kortenaer/Bremen class open ocean submarine hunters. Of well proportioned, if somewhat angular lines the Maestrale class, along with the Lupos, are the first of the modern, gas turbine boosted European or US frigates to reverse the downward trend in terms of top speed, the former being designed to achieve 32.5 knots with 6 months of hull exposure to marine encrustation. Already well-armed by Western world standards, provision exists to equip these ships with a hangar roof located close-in weapons system at some future date. The Mk 2 Otomat anti-ship missiles with which the Maestrales are equipped have demonstrated a range capability in excess of 97 nautical miles, while the Mach 2.0 Aspide (Italian version of the Sea Sparrow) air defence missile has a range of around 5.4 nautical miles.

An aft aspect of Grecale *(F571) fitting out.*

Annapolis class   Frigates

HMCS Annapolis *(FFH265) steaming in Atlantic waters.*

Role: Anti-submarine.   **Builders:** Various, Canada.
User: Royal Canadian Navy.
Basic data: 3,000 tons full displacement; 371 ft (113.1 m) overall length; 42 ft (12.8 m) maximum beam.   **Crew:** 228.
Propulsion: 2 English Electric geared steam turbines (total 30,000 shp); 2 propellers.
Sensors: 1 SPS-12 air search radar; 1 SPS-10 sea search and navigational radar; 1 Sperry Mk 2 fire control radar; 1 TACAN aircraft homer; 1 SQS-501, 1 SQS-503 and 1 SQS-505 hull-mounted and variable depth sonar system; automated action information data processing system.
Armament: 1 Sikorsky SH-3 Sea King helicopter; 1 twin 3-inch Mk 22 dual-purpose gun; 1 Mk 10 Limbo anti-submarine mortar; 2 triple lightweight anti-submarine torpedo tubes.
Top speed: 28 knots.   **Range:** 4,750 nautical miles at 14 knots.
Programme: This 2 ship class comprises HMCS *Annapolis* (FFH265) and HMCS *Nipigon* (FFH266). Built in Halifax Shipyards and Marine Industries, respectively, these ships both entered service during 1964, having been laid down in 1960. The Annapolis class ships, along with the 4 ship Improved Restagouche class destroyers in service with the Canadian Armed Forces, will undergo a major programme of modernisation during the next few years.
Notes: Functional, if rather unbeautiful ships, the Annapolis class are characterised by their small, side by side-mounted funnels that project from the forward end of the helicopter hangar. Air defence capability is limited for a ship of this size.

Tribal class (UK)   Frigates

KRI Martha Kristina Tiyahaku (*F331*), *1985.*

Role: General purpose.   **Builders:** Various, UK.
User: Indonesian Navy.
Basic data: 3,000 tons full displacement; 360.0 ft (109.7 m) overall length; 42.0 ft (12.8 m) maximum beam.   **Crew:** 295.
Propulsion: 1 Metrovick geared steam turbine (15,000 shp); 1 Metrovick G.6 gas turbine (7,500 shp); COSAG; 1 propeller.
Sensors: 1 Type 965 long range air search radar; 1 Type 993 low-level air and sea search radar; 1 Type 978 navigational radar; 2 Type 262 and 1 Type 963 fire control radars; 1 Type 162, 1 Type 170B and 1 Type 177 hull-mounted sonars; 1 Type 199 towed variable depth sonar (F117 and F122 only).
Armament: 1 Westland Wasp helicopter; 2 single 4.5 inch Mk 5 dual-purpose guns; 2 quadruple Sea Cat point air defence missile launchers; 2 single 20 mm anti-aircraft guns; 1 triple-barrel Limbo Mk 10 anti-submarine mortar.
Top speed: 24 knots.   **Range:** 4,500 nautical miles at 12 knots.
Programme: Originally a 7 ship class, the Type 81 frigates were completed between November 1961 and April 1964. All were modernised, including the incorporation of helipad and hangar, between 1967 and 1974. In 1983, the 3 remaining ships were sold to Indonesia. The former *Zulu* is now KRI *Martha Kristina Tiyahahu* (F331), while *Gurkha* is now KRI *Wilhelmus Sakarias Johannes* (F332) and *Tartar* has re-emerged as KRI *Hasanuddin* (F333).
Notes: Of deceptively conventional appearance, the Tribal class was, in fact, made up of the first series built warships to employ a combined steam and gas turbine (COSAG) propulsion arrangement. The Wasp helicopter is stowed in its below helipad hangar at a right angle to the ship's fore-and-aft axis.

Improved Restagouche class   Frigates

An aft aspect of HMCS Terra Nova *(FF259), showing the ASROC missile-launcher and stern variable depth sonar.*

Role: Anti-submarine.   **Builders:** Various, Canada.
User: Royal Canadian Navy.
Basic data: 2,900 tons full displacement; 371.0 ft (113.1 m) overall length; 42.0 ft (12.8 m) maximum beam.   **Crew:** 214.
Propulsion: 2 English Electric geared steam turbines (total 30,000 shp); 2 propellers.
Sensors: 1 SPS-12 long-range air search radar; 1 SPS-10 low-level air and sea search radar; 1 Sperry Mk 2 sea search and navigational radar; 1 SPG-48 fire control radar; 1 SQS-501 and SQS-503 hull-mounted sonar and 1 SQS-505 variable depth sonar; naval tactical information system.
Armament: 1 twin 3-inch Mk 6 dual-purpose gun; 1 octuple ASROC anti-submarine missile launcher; 1 triple-barrelled Mk 10 Limbo anti-submarine rocket launcher.
Top speed: 28 knots.   **Range:** 4,750 nautical miles at 14 knots.
Programme: originally a 7-ship class, 4 remain in operational use comprising: HMCS *Gatineau* (FF236), HMCS *Restagouche* (FF257), HMCS *Kootenay* (FF258) and HMCS *Terra Nova* (FF259); all of these entering service between June 1958 and June 1959. An additional unmodified member of the class, HMCS *Columbia* (FF260) is still in use as a stationary training vessel. All 4 Improved Restagouche frigates are currently undergoing a major life extension refurbishment.
Notes: Retrofitted with SQS-505 variable depth sonar systems between 1968 and 1973, involving modifying and lengthening the vessels' sterns, all four of these ships currently serve with the Royal Canadian Navy's Pacific coast-based Second Canadian Destroyer Squadron. The current destroyer life extension (DELEX) programme on these frigates is scheduled for completion by 1986.

McKenzie class

The Royal Canadian Navy's lead of class HMCS McKenzie *(FF261).*

Role: Anti-submarine.
User: Royal Canadian Navy.
Builders: Various, Canada.
Basic data: 2,890 tons full displacement; 366.0 ft (111.6 m) overall length; 42.0 ft (12.8 m) maximum beam.
Crew: 210.
Propulsion: 2 English Electric geared steam turbines (total 30,000 shp); 2 propellers.
Sensors: 1 SPS-12 long-range air search radar; 1 SPS-10 low-level air and sea search radar; 1 Sperry Mk 2 sea search and navigational radar; 1 SPG-34 and 1 SPG-48 fire control radars; 1 SQS-501 and 1 SQS-503 hull-mounted sonars; naval tactical information system.
Armament: 2 twin 3-inch Mk 34 dual-purpose guns; 2 triple-barrelled Mk 10 Limbo anti-submarine mortars; 2 triple Mk 32 lightweight anti-submarine torpedo tubes.
Top speed: 28 knots.
Range: 4,750 nautical miles at 14 knots.
Programme: This 4-ship class comprises: HMCS *McKenzie* (FF261), HMCS *Saskatchewan* (FF262), HMCS *Yukon* (FF263) and HMCS *Qu'Appelle* (FF264). Built by four different shipbuilders, this class were laid down between December 1958 and January 1960 and all entered service between October 1962 and September 1963. Currently undergoing major modernisation.
Notes: Although relegated to serve with the Royal Canadian Navy's Pacific coast Training Group, all four ships of this class are currently undergoing a life extension refurbishment programme, including the retrofitting of new SQS-505 in place of the existing SQS-503 sonar systems.

HMS Andromeda *(F57) one of the much modified refitted Batch III Exocet and Sea Wolf-equipped ships.*

Role: Anti-submarine.
Builders: Various UK, Indian and Dutch.
Users: Navies of India, Netherlands, New Zealand and UK.
Basic data: 2,860 tons full displacement; 373 ft (113.7 m) overall length; 41 ft (12.5 m) or 43 ft (13.1 m) maximum beam on last 10 UK and 6 Indian ships.   **Crew:** c. 260.
Propulsion: 2 White E-E geared steam turbines (total 30,000 shp); 2 propellers.
Sensors: 1 Type 965 long-range air search radar on gun and Exocet equipped ships or 1 Type 993 low altitude air search radar on Ikara ships; 2 Type 903 Seacat fire control radars; 1 Type 975 or 978 sea search and navigational radar; 1 Type 177 or 184 hull-mounted and 1 Type 162, 170B or 199 towed variable depth sonar (deleted from some ships); Ferranti CAAIS automated action information data processing.
Armament: 1 Westland Wasp or Lynx helicopter; 1 twin 4.5 inch Mk 6 dual-purpose gun, or 4 Exocet anti-ship missile launchers, or 1 Ikara anti-submarine missile launcher, or 1 sextuple Sea Wolf rapid response close-in air defence missile launcher and 4 Exocet (with the exception of the Sea Wolf ships, all carry 6 cell Seacat point air defence missile launchers, gun equipped ships having 1, Ikara ships having 2 and Exocet ships carrying 3); Ikara and Exocet ships have 2 single 40 mm anti-aircraft guns, while gun equipped ships have 2 single 20 mm anti-aircraft guns; 1 treble barrelled Limbo Mk 10 anti-submarine mortar (deleted from Exocet ships, which carry 2 triple lightweight anti-submarine torpedo tubes).
Top speed: 28.5 knots.   **Range:** Up to 5,500 nautical miles at 12 knots.
Programme: All 26 Royal Navy ships were commissioned between

March 1963 and February 1973. Having undergone extensive refits, the ships fall into 3 categories: the Ikara group, comprising HMS *Leander* (F109), HMS *Ajax* (F114), HMS *Aurora* (F10), HMS *Euryalus* (F15), HMS *Galatea* (F18), HMS *Arethusa* (F38), HMS *Naiad* (F39) and HMS *Dido* (F104); the Exocet group, comprising HMS *Cleopatra* (F28), HMS *Minerva* (F45), HMS *Phoebe* (F42), HMS *Sirius* (F40), HMS *Argonaut* (F56), HMS *Juno* (F52), HMS *Danae* (F47) and HMS *Penelope* (F127); and the Broad-Beamed group, originally gun-equipped being converted into Sea Wolf ships, comprising HMS *Andromeda* (F57), HMS *Scylla* (F71), HMS *Hermione* (F58), HMS *Achilles* (F12), HMS *Jupiter* (F60), HMS *Diomede* (F16), HMS *Bacchante* (F69), HMS *Apollo* (F70), HMS *Charybdis* (F75) and HMS *Ariadne* (F72). The 2 British-built New Zealand vessels, HMNZS *Waikato* (F55) and HMNZS *Canterbury* (F421), were accepted 1966 and 1971, respectively. Two Dutch shipyards built 6 ships known as Van Speijk class, all accepted into service between 1967 and 1968. Six more were locally built in India between 1972 and 1980, while 2 British-built ships were delivered to Chile in December 1973 and May 1974. The former Royal Navy ships, HMS *Dido* and *Bacchante* (still gun-equipped) have been transferred to the Royal New Zealand Navy as HMNZS *Southland* and *Wellington*, respectively; HMNZS *Waikato* having been withdrawn from service.

Notes: A development of the Rothesay class frigates. All Seawolf ships carry a 6 cell Sea Wolf launcher in place of the gun turret and are fitted with Type 967/968 search radar and GWS 25 tracking radar.

The Ikara-equipped HMS Leander *(F109).*

Van Speijk class   Frigates

The lead of class, HMNLS Van Speijk *(F802), photographed in 1981 following the installation of its forward OTO-Melara gun.*

Role: General purpose.   **Builders:** Various, Netherlands.
User: Royal Netherlands Navy.
Basic data: 2,835 tons full displacement; 372.0 ft (113.4 m) overall length; 41.0 ft (12.5 m) maximum beam.   **Crew:** 180.
Propulsion: 2 Werkspoor-built English Electric geared steam turbines (total 30,000 shp); 2 propellers.
Sensors: 1 Hollandse LW 08 long range air search radar; 1 Hollandse DA 05/2 combined low-level air and sea search radar; 1 Decca 1226 sea search and navigational radar; 2 Hollandse M 44 fire control radars for Seacat and 1 Hollandse M 45 gunfire control radar; 2 separate Hollandse hull-mounted sonar systems; Hollandse SEWACO automated action information data processing system.
Armament: 1 Westland Lynx helicopter; 2 twin Harpoon anti-ship missile launchers; 2 quadruple Seacat point air defence missile launchers; 1 single 76 mm OTO-Melara compact dual-purpose gun; 2 triple Mk 32 lightweight anti-submarine torpedo tubes.
Top speed: 28 knots.   **Range:** 4,500 nautical miles at 12 knots.
Programme: This 6-ship class comprises: HMNLS *Van Speijk* (F802), HMNLS *Van Galen* (F803), HMNLS *Tjerk Hiddes* (F804), HMNLS *Van Nes* (F805), HMNLS *Isacc Sweers* (F814) and HMNLS *Evertsen* (F815). All entered service between February 1967 and August 1968. The ships were modernised and re-gunned between 1977 and 1981.
Notes: The Van Speijk class started life as Dutch-built and sensored versions of the broad-beamed or Group III Leander class frigates, carrying an extra Seacat missile launcher compared to their Royal Navy contemporaries.

Whitby and River classes

Frigates

The South African Navy's President Pretorius *(F145).*

Role: Anti-submarine.　　　**Builders:** Various, UK and Australian.
Users: Navies of Australia (4), India (2) and South Africa (2).
Basic data: 2,800 tons full displacement; 370.0 ft (112.8 m) overall
length; 41.0 ft (12.5 m) maximum beam.　　　**Crew:** around 210.
Propulsion: 2 geared steam turbines (total 30,000 shp); 2 propellers.
Sensors: 1 Hollandse LWO-2 (Australian) or Thomson-CSF Jupiter
(South African) long-range air search radar; 1 Type 298 height finder
radar; 1 Type 978 sea search and navigational radar; 1 Hollandse M 22
(Australian) or ELSAG NA 9C (South African) gunfire control radar;
1 each of various British hull-mounted and variable depth sonars as
original fit.
Armament: 1 Wasp helicoper (South African only); 1 twin 4.5 inch
Mk 6 dual-purpose gun; 1 quadruple Seacat point air defence missile
launcher (Australian only); 2 single 40 mm Bofors anti-aircraft guns
(South African only); 1 Ikara anti-submarine missile launcher (Aus-
tralian only) or 1 triple Mk 10 Limbo anti-submarine mortar (South
African only); 1 triple lightweight anti-submarine torpedo tube (South
African) or 2 triple torpedo tubes refitted to Australian, except F45.
Top speed: 29 knots.　　　**Range:** 4,500 nautical miles at 12 knots.
Programme: A total of 14 ships of this basic Type 12 AS class were
built; 4 for the Royal Navy, 4 locally-built for Australia, plus 6
British-built for export to India, New Zealand and South Africa. All
delivered between 1956 and 1964, the 8 ships remaining in service
comprise: the Royal Australian Navy's *Yarra* (F45), *Parramatta* (F46),
Stuart (F48) and *Derwent* (F49), India's *Talwar* (F40) and *Trishul*
(F43), along with the South African Navy's *President Pretorius* (F145)
and *President Steyn* (F147); a 3rd ship *President Kruger* was lost in
early 1982.
Notes: All remaining examples are much modified variants of the original Whitby design.

HMAS Torrens *(F53), one of two Improved River class ships.*

Role: Anti-submarine.   **Builders:** Various, Australia.
User: Royal Australian Navy.
Basic data: 2,750 tons full displacement; 370 ft (112.8 m) overall
length; 41 ft (12.5 m) maximum beam.   **Crew:** 250.
Propulsion: 2 geared steam turbines (total 30,400 shp); 2 propellers.
Sensors: 1 Hollandse LWO2 long-range air search radar; 1 sea search
and navigational radar; 2 Hollandse M22 fire control radars; 3 sonars
(Type 162, 170 and 177).
Armament: 1 twin 4.5 inch Mk 6 dual-purpose gun; 1 Ikara anti-
submarine missile launcher; 1 twin Seacat point air defence missile
launcher; 1 Limbo anti-submarine mortar; 6 lightweight anti-submarine
torpedo tubes.
Top speed: 27 knots.   **Range:** 4,500 nautical miles at 12 knots.
Programme: During the early 1960s, 4 River class frigates were built
by the naval Dockyard at Williamstown and the Cockatoo Island yard at
Sydney. These ships, HMAS *Yarra* (F45), HMAS *Parramatta* (F46),
HMAS *Stuart* (F48) and HMAS *Derwent* (F49), were based on the
Royal Navy's Rothesay class. This quartet was followed some 6 years
on by HMAS *Swan* (F50) and HMAS *Torrens* (F53), built by the
Naval Dockyard and Cockatoo and commissioned in January 1970
and January 1971, respectively.
Notes: The Improved River class ships, although marginally shorter,
closely resemble the Royal Navy's Leander class ships.

St Laurent class

HMCS Fraser *(F233). Note the stern-mounted variable depth sonar installation.*

Role: Anti-submarine.   **Builders:** Various, Canada.
User: Royal Canadian Navy.
Basic data: 2,850 tons full displacement; 366.0 ft (111.5 m) overall length; 42.0 ft (12.8 m) maximum beam.   **Crew:** 218.
Propulsion: 2 English Electric geared steam turbines (total 30,000 shp); 2 propellers.
Sensors: 1 SPS-12 air search radar; 1 SPS-10 sea search and navigational radar; 1 SPG-48 gun fire control radar; 1 TACAN aircraft homer; SQS-501, -503 and -505 hull-mounted and variable depth sonar system; naval tactical information data processing.
Armament: 1 Sea King helicopter; 1 twin 3 inch Mk 33 anti-aircraft gun; 2 triple lightweight anti-submarine torpedo tubes; 1 triple-barrelled Mk 10 Limbo depth charge launcher.
Top speed: 28 knots.   **Range:** 4,750 nautical miles at 14 knots.
Programme: Originally a 7 ship class comprising: HMCS *St Laurent* (F205), HMCS *Saquenay* (F206), HMCS *Ottawa* (F229), HMCS *Margaree* (F230), HMCS *Fraser* (F233) and HMCS *Assiniboine* (F324). All were laid down between April 1951 and May 1952, the class entering service between November 1956 and October 1957. The lead ship, *St Laurent*, was withdrawn from service during 1974.
Notes: An innovative enough design when it first appeared in the early 1950s, the St Laurent class continued the Royal Canadian Navy's pioneering developments in anti-submarine warfare, when, in the 1963 to 1966 period, all 7 ships underwent a major modernisation to add the elevated helipad/hangar complex and variable depth sonar.

Pedar Skram class

Frigates

The Royal Danish Navy ship Herlaf Trolle (*F353*).

Role: General purpose.   **Builder:** Helsinger Vaerft, Denmark.
User: Royal Danish Navy.
Basic data: 2,720 tons full displacement; 369.1 ft (112.5 m) overall length; 39.4 ft (12.0 m) maximum beam.   **Crew:** 200.
Propulsion: 2 Pratt & Whitney GG4A-3 gas turbines (total 44,000 shp) or 2 General Motors 16-567D diesels (total 4,800 bhp); CODOG; 2 controllable-pitch propellers.
Sensors: 1 CWS-2 long range air search radar; 1 CWS-3 combined low-level air/sea search radar; 1 Scanter 009 sea search and navigational radar; 3 M 40 gun fire control radars; 2 Mk 91 fire control radars (Sea Sparrow); 1 Plessey MS 26 hull-mounted sonar; CEPLO automated action information data processing system.
Armament: 8 Harpoon anti-ship missile launchers; 1 octuple Sea Sparrow point air defence missile launcher; 1 twin 5 inch Mk 12 dual-purpose gun; 4 single 40 mm Bofors anti-aircraft guns; 4 heavy-weight anti-submarine torpedo tubes; 1 depth charge rack.
Top speed: 28 knots.   **Range:** 3,900 nautical miles at 14 knots.
Programme: This 2 ship class comprises: *Pedar Skram* (F352) and *Herlaf Trolle* (F353). These sister ships were laid down in September and December of 1964, with service entry dates of June 1966 and April 1967, respectively. Underwent modernisation during the 1977–79 period.
Notes: The Pedar Skram design has an extremely seaworthy hull, a relatively capable and balanced weapons fit and a massive twin funnel-dominated superstructure.

The lead of class Alpino *(F580).*

Role: General purpose. **Builder:** CNR, Italy.
User: Italian Navy.
Basic data: 2,698 tons full displacement; 371.6 ft (113.25 m) overall length; 43.6 ft (13.3 m) maximum beam. **Crew:** 254.
Propulsion: 2 CNR-built Metrovick G6 gas turbines (total 15,400 shp) and 4 Tosi OTV-320 diesels (total 16,800 bhp); CODAG; 2 propellers.
Sensors: 1 SPS-12 air search radar; 1 SPQ-2 low-level air/sea search and navigational radar; 2 Selenia/Elsag RTN-10X fire control radars; 1 SQS-43 hull-mounted sonar; 1 SQA-10 towed variable depth sonar.
Armament: 2 Agusta-Bell AB 204 or 212 helicopters; 6 single 76 mm dual-purpose guns; 1 single 305 mm Menon anti-submarine mortar; 2 triple Elsag-built Mk 32 lightweight anti-submarine torpedo tubes.
Top speed: 29 knots. **Range:** 5,070 nautical miles at 18 knots.
Programme: This 2 ship class comprises: *Alpino* (F580) and *Caribiniere* (F581). The frigates were laid down in February 1963 and January 1965, entering service in January and April 1968, respectively.
Notes: The first warships anywhere in the world to be designed around a combined diesel and gas (CODAG) propulsion machinery arrangement, the Alpino class can achieve speeds of up to 20 knots under diesel power alone. Both helicopters cannot be operated simultaneously.

Madina class   Frigates

The Royal Saudi Arabian ship Madina (*F702*).

Role: General purpose.   **Builders:** DCAN and CNIM, France.
User: Royal Saudi Arabian Navy.
Basic data: 2,610 tons full displacement; 377.3 ft (115.0 m) overall
length; 41.0 ft (12.5 m) maximum beam.   **Crew:** 179.
Propulsion: 4 SEMT-Pielstick 16 PA 6BTC diesels (total
35,200 bhp); 2 propellers.
Sensors: 1 Thomson-CSF Sea Tiger (DRBV 15) air search radar with
IFF; 2 Racal-Decca 1226 sea search and navigational radars; 1
Thomson-CSF Castor II primary missile/gun fire control radar; 1
Thomson-CSF DRBC 32E fire control radar for Crotale; 1 Thomson-
CSF Diodin hull-mounted sonar; 1 Thomson-CSF Sorel variable depth
sonar; 3 CSEE Naja optronic fire direction systems; Thomson-CSF
SENIT VI automated action information data processing system; 1
CSEE Sylosat precision position fixing system.
Armament: 1 Aerospatiale AS 365F Dauphin 2 helicopter; 8 Otomat
Mk 2 anti-ship missile launchers; 1 single 100 mm Creusot Loire com-
pact dual-purpose gun; 1 octuple Naval Crotale point air defence mis-
sile launcher; 2 twin 40 mm Breda/Bofors anti-aircraft guns; 4 heavyweight anti-submarine torpedo tubes.
Top speed: 30 knots.   **Range:** 6,500 nautical miles at 15 knots.
Programme: The Saudi Arabian Government ordered 4 of these
F2000S design ships as part of the multi-system Sawari Contract
ratified in early October 1980. The lead vessel, *Madina* (F702) was
laid down in the yards of DCAN, Lorient in mid-October 1981,
launched in April 1982 and was delivered during March 1984. The remaining 3 frigates, *Hofouf* (F704), *Abha* (F706) and *Taif* (F708), are

currently being fitted out in CNIM, La Seyne yards where they were built, and should all be delivered by the latter half of 1985.

Notes: Although undoubtedly expensive ships, the Medina class frigates are amongst the best sensored and armed ships of their size, certainly in terms of anti-ship and anti-submarine capability. Much more significantly, the total weapons systems concept, that is the vessel, its equipment and support programme in terms of logistics and training, are all attuned to the specific user's requirements, which is, perhaps one of the underlying reasons why the Saudi Arabians selected this particular Thomson-CSF-managed programme instead of the rival Italian submission. In terms of the Medina class vessels' armament, it is of interest to make a direct comparison between these ships and the larger Georges Leygues destroyers, for, with the exception of a second onboard helicopter, the Medina design can muster more throw-weight than their larger brethren, particularly in the area of close-in anti-air firepower, thanks largely to their fire-directed pair of Breda/Bofors twin gun mounts.

Madina (*F702*). *Note Crotale launcher just forward of helicopter hangar.*

The Italian Navy's Sagittario *(F565).*

Role: General purpose.   **Builder:** CNR, Italy.
Users: Navies of Italy (4), Iraq (4), Peru (4) and Venezuela (6).
Basic data: 2,525 tons full displacement: 371.4 ft (113.2 m) overall
length; 37.1 ft (11.8 m) maximum beam.   **Crew:** 185.
Propulsion: 2 General Electric LM2500 gas turbines (total
50,000 shp) or 2 GMT A320-20M diesels (total 8,490 bhp); CODOG;
2 controllable pitch propellers.
Sensors: 1 Selenia RAN-10S primary air/sea search radar; 1 Selenia
RAN-11XL close-in air/sea search and navigational radar; 2 Selenia
RTN-10X fire control radars (missile); 2 ELSAG NA-10 fire control
radars (guns); 1 Raytheon 1160B hull-mounted sonar; Selenia IPN-10
automated action information data processing.
Armament: 1 Agusta-Bell 212 helicopter; 8 Otomat Mk 2 anti-ship
missile launchers; 1 OTO-Melara 127 mm dual-purpose gun; 1 octuple
Aspide medium-range air defence missile launcher; 2 twin Breda/
Bofors 40 mm anti-aircraft guns; 2 triple lightweight anti-submarine
torpedo tubes.
Top speed: 35 knots.   **Range:** 4,350 nautical miles at 16 knots.
Programme: Ordered between 1974 and 1977, the 4 Italian frigates
comprise: *Lupo* (F564), *Sagittario* (F565), *Perseo* (F566) and *Orsa*
(F567), the ships entering service in September 1977, November 1978,
February 1979 and March 1980, respectively. In 1974, Peru ordered 4
examples of this class comprising: *Meliton Carvajal* (F51), *Villavicencio*
(F52), both built by CNR and delivered by mid-1979, while SIMA in
Peru were responsible for the building of *Montero* (F53) and F54, the

former being launched in 1982. In October 1975, the Venezuelan Government placed contracts for 6, all to be built in Italy. *Mariscal Sucre* (F21), the first of the Venezuelan ships, entered service in November 1979, followed by *Almirante Brion* (F22) in 1980 and *General Urdaneta* (F23) in 1981. All 3 remaining ships, *General Soublette* (F24), *General Salom* (F25) and *Jose Felix Ribas* (F26) (re-named *Almirante de Garcia*), had been delivered by the close of 1982. In February 1981, Iraq contracted for 4 of these ships, *Hittin* (F14), *Thi Qar* (F15), *Alqadisyya* (F16) and *Alyrmook* (F17), the first of which entered trials in April 1984.

Notes: Notable for its success in the export market place, the Lupo class has proved to be the largest single frigate construction programme outside the US. While the primary armament of the Lupo class vessels remains the same in all cases, there are a number of layout variations that help to distinguish the ships of each navy. In the case of both Peruvian and Venezuelan vessels there is an open quarter deck below the stern-mounted helicopter flight pad, while the Peruvian vessels employ a fixed as opposed to the telescoping hangar of the parent Lupo class.

Venezuela's Almirante de Garcia (*F26*) *on sea trials.*

Wielingen class

Frigates

The Royal Belgian Navy ship Westdiep (*F911*).

Role: General purpose.
Builder: Boelwerf & Cockerill, Belgium.
User: Royal Belgian Navy.
Basic data: 2,283 tons full displacement; 349 ft (106.4 m) overall length; 40.4 ft (12.3 m) maximum beam.   **Crew:** 160.
Propulsion: 1 Rolls-Royce TM3B Olympus gas turbine (28,000 shp) or 2 Cockerill CO-240V-12 diesels (total 6,000 bhp); CODOG; 2 controllable-pitch propellers.
Sensors: 1 Hollandse DA 05 combined air and sea search radar; 1 Raytheon TM 1645/9X sea search and navigational radar; 1 Hollandse WM-25 fire control radar; 1 Canadian SQS-505A hull and towed variable depth sonar; Hollandse SEWACO automated action information data processor.
Armament: 4 Exocet anti-ship missile launchers; 1 single 100 mm dual-purpose gun; 1 octuple Sea Sparrow point air defence missile launcher; 2 single 20 mm anti-aircraft guns; 2 single heavyweight anti-submarine torpedo launchers; 1 sextuple 375 mm Bofors anti-submarine rocket launcher.
Top speed: 28 knots.   **Range:** 5,000 nautical miles at 14 knots.
Programme: This 4 ship class comprises *Wielingen* (F910), *Westdiep* (F911), *Wandelaar* (F912) and *Westhinder* (F913). Laid down between March 1974 and December 1975, they commissioned in March 1976, June 1977 and October 1978 for 3rd and 4th ships.
Notes: These vessels have no helicopter facilities and are characterised by their low superstructure and relatively massive funnel.

Yugoslavian frigate

The Iraqi Navy's Ibn Khaldum *(F507)* prior to delivery.

Role: General purpose/training.   **Builder:** Uljanic, Yugoslavia.
Users: Navies of Iraq, Indonesia and Yugoslavia.
Basic data: 2,050 tons full displacement; 317.3 ft (96.7 m) overall length; 36.7 ft (11.2 m) maximum beam.   **Crew:** 76.
Propulsion: 1 Rolls-Royce TM3B Olympus (28,400 shp) or 2 MTU 16V956 TB91 diesels (total 7,500 bhp); CODOG; 2 controllable-pitch propellers.
Sensors: 1 Philips (Sweden) 9GR 600 combined low-level air/sea search radar; 2 Kelvin Hughes sea search and navigational radars; 1 Philips (Sweden) 9LV200 Mk II gun fire control and automated action information data processing system; 1 hull-mounted sonar.
Armament: 4 MM 40 Exocet anti-ship missile launchers (Iraqi only) or 1 aft helipad (Indonesian only); 1 single 57 mm Bofors SAK 57 Mk 1 dual-purpose gun; 1 single 40 mm Bofors D70 and 4 quadruple 20 mm M75 anti-aircraft guns; 1 depth charge mortar and depth charge rail.
Top speed: 26 knots.   **Range:** 4,000 nautical miles at 18 knots.
Programme: A 5 ship class comprising the Iraqi *Ibn Khaldum* (F507), delivered in March 1980, plus Indonesia's *Hadjar Bewantoro* (F364) and an unidentified sister. The 1st of 2 for Yugoslavia was laid down during 1981.
Notes: The hull is of welded mild steel, while the ship has a light alloy superstructure. The related pair of Yugoslavian frigates are reported to use a Soviet-developed gas turbine and to employ a CODAG arrangement, driving 3 propellers.

Koni class   Frigates

The Yugoslavian-operated Split *(F31) seen from abeam as delivered.*

Role: General purpose.   **Builder:** Zelenodolsk, USSR.
Users: Navies of USSR, Algeria, Cuba, East Germany and Yugoslavia.
Basic data: 1,980 tons full displacement; 315.0 ft (96.0 m) overall
length; 39.4 ft (12.0 m) maximum beam.   **Crew:** Around 130.
Propulsion: 1 gas turbine (15,000 shp) and 2 diesels (total
15,000 bhp); CODAG; 3 propellers.
Sensors: 1 air search radar; 1 sea search and navigational radar; 1
missile fire control radar; 1 each fire control radars for 76.2 mm and
30 mm weapons; 1 hull-mounted sonar; automated action information
system.
Armament: 4 SS-N-2B Styx anti-ship missile launchers (on Yugoslavian ships only); 1 twin SA-N-4 point air defence missile launcher;
2 twin 76.2 mm dual-purpose guns; 2 twin 30 mm anti-aircraft
guns; 2 twelve-barrelled 250 mm RBU-6000 anti-submarine rocket
launchers; depth charges; mines.
Top speed: 28 knots.   **Range:** In excess of 2,000 nautical miles at
20 knots.
Programme: Apparently developed specifically for export to Soviet
client nations, 7 Koni class vessels had been positively identified by
mid-1983, comprising: the sole Soviet *Timofey Ul'yantsev*, the East
German pair *Rostock* (F141) and *Berlin* (F142), Algeria's *Mourad Rais*
(901), Cuba's *Mariel* and the Yugoslavian *Split* (F31) and as yet to be
identified F32. Initial deliveries of the Koni class commenced in 1978,
with construction of these vessels continuing in the early 1980s at
around 1 ship per year.
Notes: Somewhat larger than the current Soviet submarine chasing
Petya Grisha or Mirka classes.

Jianghu class   Frigates

514, *a Jianghu class missile frigate showing its low profile.*

Role: General purpose.   **Builder:** Jiangnan Shipyards, China.
User: Chinese People's Republic Navy.
Basic data: 1,900 tons full displacement; 338.6 ft (103.2 m) overall
length; 33.5 ft (10.2 m) maximum beam.   **Crew:** 195.
Propulsion: 2 Pielstick diesels (total 16,000 bhp); 2 propellers.
Sensors: 1 combined low-level air and sea search radar; 1 sea search
and missile fire control radar; 1 sea search and navigational radar; 1
hull-mounted sonar; tactical information system.
Armament: 2 twin SS-N-2 Styx anti-ship missile launchers; 2
single 100 mm dual-purpose guns; 4 twin 37 mm anti-aircraft guns; 2
five-barrelled 250 mm RBU-1200 anti-submarine rocket launchers; 2
depth charge projectors; 2 depth charge racks; mines.
Top speed: 26 knots.   **Range:** 4,000 nautical miles at 20 knots.
Programme: Reported as having been initially deployed in 1975, at
least 11 of this class were thought to be in service by early 1982 with
2 more being built.
Notes: A very workmanlike design that appears to employ steel construction throughout both hull and superstructure. The primary anti-
ship armament of SS-N-2 Styx missiles is mounted on swivelling
launchers similar to those fitted to the larger Luta class destroyers
operated by the Chinese. At least one of this class, *533*, sports an
oval-sectioned funnel in place of the rectangular-sectioned type de-
picted in the accompanying photograph.

The lead ship Almirante Padilla (*F51*) *during its 1982 sea trials.*

Role: General purpose.
Builder: Howaldtswerke, Federal Germany.
Users: Navies of Colombia (4) and Malaysia (2).
Basic data: 1,700 tons full displacement; 312.75 ft (95.3 m) overall length; 37.0 ft (11.3 m) maximum beam (Colombian ships): 1900 tons full displacement; 319.2 ft (97.3 m) overall length; 37.0 ft (11.3 m) maximum beam (Malaysian ships).   **Crew:** Around 88.
Propulsion: 4 MTU 20V1163 diesels (total 23,000 bhp); 2 controllable-pitch propellers.
Sensors: 1 of various unidentified combined low-level air/sea search radar; 1 unidentified sea search and navigational radar; 1 unidentified fire control radar; 1 unidentified hull-mounted sonar; unidentified automated action information data processing system.
Armament: 1 Lynx-sized helicopter; 8 (Colombian) or 4 (Malaysian) MM 40 Exocet anti-ship missile launchers; 1 single 100 mm model 1968 Creusot-Loire (Malaysian) or 76 mm OTO-Melara Compact (Colombian) dual-purpose gun; 1 twin 40 mm Breda/Bofors anti-aircraft (Colombian) gun; 2 twin 30 mm Emerlec anti-aircraft guns (Malaysian ships only); 2 triple lightweight anti-submarine torpedo tubes.
Top speed: 26.5 knots.   **Range:** 5,000 nautical miles at 18 knots.
Programme: 6 examples of this light frigate had been ordered by end 1985, the initial Colombian order for 4 ships having been placed in May 1980, followed by the July 1981 Malaysian order for 2 vessels. The Colombian ships comprise: *Almirante Padilla* (F51), *Caldas* (F52), *Antioquia* (F53) and *Independiente* (F54). Launched in January 1982, F51, the lead ship, commenced sea trials in July 1982 and all of the Colombian vessels were delivered before the close of 1984. The Royal Malaysian Navy frigates comprise: *Kasturi* (F25) and *Lekir* (F26), both delivered in August 1984.

Notes: Designed for their weapons load carrying ability, coupled to long mission endurance, rather than against a requirement calling for a high speed vessel, the forward superstructure of the two nations' ships varies considerably, as do their weapons fit. The sale of these frigates represents a major commercial success for Howaldtswerke-Deutsche Werft, well established as the supplier of the Type 209 classes of submarine, but previously totally unknown in the highly competitive market for frigate designs. The quite different weapons fits selected by the two customer navies reflect Colombia's primary anti-shipping priorities, versus Malaysia's interest in naval bombardment and anti-air missions.

Malaysia's lead of class Kasturi (F25), *equipped with its 100 mm Creusot-Loire compact gun.*

KNM Bergen (F301), with 3 of its 6 Penguin anti-ship missile launchers visible beneath the stern flagpole.

Role: General purpose.
Builder: Royal Norwegian Naval Dockyards.
User: Royal Norwegian Navy.
Basic data: 1,850 tons full displacement; 317.0 ft (96.62 m) overall length; 36.65 ft (11.17 m) maximum beam. **Crew:** 150.
Propulsion: 1 STAL-Laval PN 20 geared steam turbine (20,000 shp); 1 propeller.
Sensors: 1 DRBV 22 air search radar; 1 Decca TM 1226 sea search and navigational radar; 1 Hollandse M 22 fire control radar; 1 Mk 91 Sea Sparrow fire control radar; 1 SQS-36 hull-mounted sonar; 1 each search and attack hull-mounted sonars for Terne system; automated action information data processing system.
Armament: 1 octuple Sea Sparrow point air defence missile launcher; 6 Penguin anti-ship missile launchers; 2 twin 3-inch Mk 33 anti-aircraft guns; 1 single 200 mm Terne anti-submarine rocket launcher; 2 single lightweight anti-submarine torpedo tubes.
Top speed: 25 knots. **Range:** 4,500 nautical miles at 15 knots.
Programme: This 5 ship class comprises: *Oslo* (F300), *Bergen* (F301), *Trondheim* (F302), *Stavanger* (F303) and *Narvik* (F304). All laid down in the 1963/64 period, the ships were completed between January 1966 and December 1967.
Notes: Although employing the hull, propulsive machinery and basic weapons fit of the US Navy's Dealey class design, the Oslo class incorporate a number of significant improvements in terms of their sensors and weapons fit.

Riga class

A Soviet-operated Riga class.

Role: Anti-submarine.
Builders: Various, USSR and Chinese People's Republic.
Users: Navies of USSR, Bulgaria, Chinese People's Republic and Finland.
Basic data: 1,480 tons full displacement; 298.6 ft (91.0 m) overall length; 36.1 ft (11.0 m) maximum beam.   **Crew:** Around 175.
Propulsion: 2 geared steam turbines (total 20,000 shp); 2 propellers.
Sensors: 1 combined low-level air/sea search and navigational radar; 3 IFF; 2 separate fire control radars form 100 mm and anti-aircraft guns; 1 hull-mounted sonar.
Armament: 3 single 100 mm dual-purpose guns; 2 twin 37 mm and 2 twin 25 mm anti-aircraft guns (2 single 40 mm; 1 twin 30 mm Gatling type and 2 single 20 mm anti-aircraft guns on Finnish ship); 2 sixteen-barrelled 150 mm RBU 2500 anti-submarine rocket launchers; 2 or 3 heavyweight anti-submarine torpedo tubes; 2 racks of depth charges (Finnish ship has had all anti-submarine weaponry deleted); mines.
Top speed: 30 knots.   **Range:** 550 nautical miles at 28 knots.
Programme: Around 64 Riga class ships were built in Soviet shipyards between 1952 and 1958, while another 4 were built in China between 1954 and 1957. Currently, around 35 still remain in service with the Soviet Navy. Other Riga class ships still in service are the 2 Bulgarian vessels *Druzkiy* and *Smely*, the 4 Chinese ships, along with Finland's *Hameemaa* (F02).
Notes: Built as light escort/anti-submarine vessels during the 1950s.

Ishikari class   Frigates

Ishikari (*F226*), *lead ship of this three frigate class.*

Role: General purpose.   **Builders:** Various, Japan.
User: Japanese Maritime Self-Defence Force.
Basic data: 1,450 tons (F226) or 1,690 tons (F227, F228) full displacement; 277.2 ft (84.5 m) for F226 or 298.6 ft (91.0 m) for F227, F228 overall length; 32.8 ft (10.0 m) for F226 or 35.4 ft (10.8 m) for F227, F228 maximum beam.   **Crew:** 90 (F226); 98 (others).
Propulsion: 1 Kawasaki-built Rolls-Royce TM3B Olympus gas turbine (28,400 shp) or 1 Mitsubishi 6DRV 35/44 diesel (4,650 bhp); CODOG; 2 controllable-pitch propellers.
Sensors: 1 OPS-28 sea search and navigational radar; 1 GFCS-2 gun and missile fire control radar; 1 unidentified hull-mounted sonar.
Armament: 2 quadruple Harpoon anti-ship missile launchers; 1 single 76 mm OTO-Melara compact dual-purpose gun; 1 Phalanx 20 mm close-in weapons system (F227, F228 only); 1 quadruple 375 mm Bofors anti-submarine rocket launcher; 2 triple 324 mm torpedo tubes.
Top speed: 25 knots.   **Range:** 4,500 nautical miles at 18 knots.
Programme: Ordered in 1977, this 3-ship class comprises: the semi-definitive *Ishikari* (F226), plus the larger *Yubari* (F227) and *Yubbetsu* (F228). The lead frigate was entered into service in March 1981, F227 being completed in March 1983 and F228 in March 1984.
Notes: Designed as a replacement for the Chikugo class frigates, the Ishikari class carries a much more potent anti-ship weapons fit than its forebears.

Petya I and II classes   Frigates

A Petya II class Soviet anti-submarine frigate.

Role: Anti-submarine.
Builders: Kaliningrad and Komsomolsk, USSR.
Users: Navies of USSR, India, Syria and Vietnam.
Basic data: 1,140 tons full displacement; 270.0 ft (82.3 m) overall length; 29.85 ft (9.1 m) maximum beam.   **Crew:** 80 to 90.
Propulsion: 2 gas turbines (total 30,000 shp) and 1 diesel (6,000 bhp); CODAG; 3 propellers.
Sensors: 1 combined air/sea search radar; 1 sea search and navigational radar; 1 gun fire control radar; 1 IFF radar; 1 dipping sonar; automated action information data processing and data links.
Armament: 2 twin 76.2 mm dual-purpose guns; 2 twelve-barrelled 250 mm RBU-6000 (Petya II) or 4 sixteen-barrelled 250 mm RBU-2500 anti-submarine rocket launchers; 2 quintuple (Petya II) or 1 quintuple (Petya I) medium anti-submarine torpedo tubes; 2 depth charge racks; mines. Note: the 1 Modified Petya II vessel carries the same weapons fit as the Petya I class ships.
Top speed: 29 knots.   **Range:** 4,000 nautical miles at 10 knots.
Programme: This 45 ship programme consists of 8 Petya Is, 26 Petya IIs, 10 Modified Petya Is and Modified Petya II. Deliveries of the Petya Is occurred between 1961 and 1964, followed by the Petya IIs from 1964 through 1969. The 10 Modified Petya II were converted in the 1973/74 period, while the sole Modified Petya I was converted during 1978.
Notes: The various Petya classes follow the established Soviet formula for submarine chaser vessels.

Espora class   Corvettes

The lead ship ARA Espora *(P4) at speed.*

Role: General purpose.   **Builder:** AFNE, Argentina.
User: Argentinian Navy.
Basic data: 1,800 tons full displacement; 299.2 ft (91.2 m) overall length; 36.0 ft (11.0 m) maximum beam.   **Crew:** 90.
Propulsion: 2 SEMT-Pielstick 16 PC2-5V400 diesels (total 22,600 bhp); 2 propellers.
Sensors: 1 Hollandse DA 05/2 combined air/sea search radar; 1 Decca TM 1226 sea search and navigational radar; 1 Hollandse WM 22 fire control radar (for Exocet and 76 mm gun); 1 Hollandse LIROD optronic fire control system (for 40 mm guns); 1 Krupp Atlas AS04 hull-mounted sonar system; EASY automated action information data processing system.
Armament: 1 Lynx sized helicopter; 8 MM 40 Exocet anti-ship missile launchers; 1 single 76 mm OTO-Melara compact dual-purpose gun; 2 twin 44 mm Breda/Bofors anti-aircraft guns; 2 triple lightweight anti-submarine torpedo tubes; 2 machine guns.
Top speed: 28 knots.   **Range:** 4,000 nautical miles at 18 knots.
Programme: Designated MEKO 140 (without hangar) and 140H (with helicopter hangar) by Blohm und Voss, the West German company received an August 1979 contract to provide design and lead yard services to Argentina, who are building 3 examples each of both variants in their own naval shipyards. The first of these Argentinian vessels, ARA *Espora* (P4) was laid down in April 1981, launched in January 1982 and entered sea trials during early 1984. *Espora* was commissioned in early July 1985 and all 6 corvettes should be in service by the close of 1986. The remaining ships comprise ARA *Rosales* (P5), ARA *Spiro* (P6), ARA *Parker* (P7), ARA *Robinson* (P8) and ARA *Seaver* (P9).

Notes: Larger and heavier than the 3 Drummond class corvettes that the Argentinians procured from France in the mid-1970s, these Blohm und Voss designed ships each packs far more anti-ship and anti-submarine weapons punch than that carried by the 13,480 ton Argentinian cruiser *General Belgrano*, lost to enemy action on 2nd May 1982. Employing the same MEKO system of readily exchangeable weapons packages as the Argentinian Navy's Almirante Brown destroyers, the Espora class corvettes can, therefore, benefit from a higher degree of fleet logistic support than could have been previously attained. As with their larger sisters, the Almirante Browns, the Espora class vessels pack a considerable close-in anti-air capability, thanks to their fire directed 40 mm gun system, known to be highly effective between 0.65 and 1.3 nautical miles (1.2 to 2.5 km). As with other members of the MEKO family of vessels, the Espora class utilises steel as the basic construction material for both hull and superstructure. Notably, while being formidable enough adversaries in terms of shipboard weapons punch relative to ship size, the addition of these 6 vessels must be seen in the broader context of other recent Argentinian naval procurement programmes. These, when taken together, will, by the latter 1980s, see the transformation of this nation's navy from that of a largely ex-US World War II-equipped force at the beginning of the 1970s into the largest and arguably best equipped navy in South America.

An aft aspect of Espora (*P4*) *on trials.*

137

Descubierta class   Corvettes

The Spanish Navy's Cazadora *(F35).*

Role: General purpose.   **Builder:** Bazan, Spain.
Users: Spanish, Moroccan and Egyptian Navies.
Basic data: 1,520 tons full displacement; 291.6 ft (88.88 m) overall
length; 34.1 ft (10.4 m) maximum beam.   **Crew:** 148.
Propulsion: 4 MTU-Bazan 16V956 TB91 diesels (total 16,000 bhp);
2 controllable-pitch propellers.
Sensors: 1 Hollandse DA-05/2 air/sea search radar; 1 Hollandse
ZW.06 sea search and navigational radar; 1 Hollandse WM-22 fire
control radar; 1 Raytheon 1160B hull-mounted sonar; 1 Raytheon 1167
towed variable depth sonar.
Armament: 2 quadruple Harpoon anti-ship missile launchers; 1 octuple Sea Sparrow point air defence missile launcher; 1 OTO-Melara
76 mm dual-purpose gun; 2 single 40 mm anti-aircraft guns; 1 twin
375 mm Bofors anti-submarine rocket launcher; 2 triple 324 mm tor-
pedo tubes.
Top speed: 26 knots.   **Range:** 6,100 nautical miles at 18 knots.
Programme: Currently a 9 ship class ordered in 2 batches of 4 Spanish ships each in 1973 and 1976, respectively, comprising: *Descubierta*
(F31), *Diana* (F32), *Infanta Elena* (F33), *Infanta Cristina* (F34),
Cazadora (F35), *Vencedora* (F36), *Centinela* (F37) and *Serviola* (F38).
Launched between 1975–80 they entered service between 1978–82.
In June 1977, Morocco ordered 1 ship, *Colonel Errhamani* (F501),
which was completed at the end of February 1983. An Egyptian order
for 2 ships was placed in September 1982, the former Spanish Navy's
F37 and F38 being transferred to Egypt in 1984 as *El Suez* (F941) and
Abuqir (F946).
Notes: The design of this class was influenced by Blohm und Voss's
Joao Coutinho class which Bazan helped to build.

Fatahillah class

Corvettes

KRI Nala (*F363*), *unique in having a helipad aft.*

Role: General purpose.

Builder: Wilton-Fijennoord, Netherlands.   **User:** Indonesian Navy.

Basic data: 1,450 tons full displacement; 275.1 ft (83.85 m) overall length; 36.4 ft (11.1 m) maximum beam.   **Crew:** 82.

Propulsion: 1 Rolls-Royce TM3B Olympus (28,000 shp) or 2 MTU 16V 956 TB91 diesels (total 4,400 bhp); CODOG; 2 controllable-pitch propellers.

Sensors: 1 Hollandse DA-05 search radar; 1 Decca AC 1229 navigational radar; 1 Hollandse WM25 fire control radar; 1 Van der Heem PHS-32 hull-mounted sonar; Hollandse automated action information.

Armament: 4 Exocet anti-ship missile launchers; 1 Bofors 120 mm gun; 1 Bofors 20 mm anti-aircraft gun: 1 Bofors twin-barrel 375 mm anti-submarine rocket launcher; 2 triple lightweight anti-submarine torpedo tubes. *Nala* only has facilities and hangar for helicopter.

Top speed: 30 knots.   **Range:** 4,250 nautical miles at 15 knots.

Programme: Ordered in August 1975, this 3 ship class comprises *Fatahillah* (F361), *Malahayati* (F362) and *Nala* (F363), all laid down between January 1977 through January 1978 and commissioned between July 1979 and summer 1980.

Notes: These modern, compact, well-armed corvettes demonstrate, once more, the recent strides made in cramming more weaponry into the minimum hull size.

Baptista de Andrade class　　　　Corvettes

The lead of class Baptista de Andrade (*F486*).

Role: Anti-submarine.　　　　　　**Builder:** Bazan, Spain.
User: Portuguese Navy.
Basic data: 1,348 tons full displacement; 277.5 ft (59.6 m) overall length; 33.8 ft (10.3 m) maximum beam.　　　　**Crew:** 113.
Propulsion: 2 OEW-Pielstick 12PC2V400 diesels (total 10,560 bhp); 2 propellers.
Sensors: 1 Plessey AWS-2 long range air search radar; 1 Decca TM 625 sea search and navigational radar; 1 Thomson-CSF Pollux gun fire control radar; 1 Thomson-CSF Diodon hull-mounted sonar.
Armament: Helipad, but no facilities to stow helicopter aboard; 1 single 100 mm Model 1968 dual-purpose gun; 2 single 40 mm Bofors anti-aircraft guns; 2 triple lightweight anti-submarine torpedo tubes; 1 depth charge rack.
Top speed: 21 knots.　　　　**Range:** 5,900 nautical miles at 18 knots.
Programme: This 4 ship class comprises: *Baptista de Andrade* (F486), *Joao Roby* (F487), *Afonso Cerqueira* (F488) and *Oliveira E. Carmo* (F489). Built in Spain, all 4 corvettes were laid down during the 1972/73 period, launched between March 1973 and February 1974, with service entry dates of November 1974, March 1975, June 1975 and February 1976, respectively.
Notes: Although modestly armed, this class, a development of the earlier Joao Coutinho class vessels designed by Blohm und Voss, have a good endurance for ships of their size, coupled to a relatively high cruising speed.

Niels Juel class

Corvettes

Niels Juel (*F354*), *with its solid, enclosed mainmast dominating.*

Role: Anti-shipping. **Builder:** Aaoborg Vaerft, Denmark.
User: Royal Danish Navy.
Basic data: 1,320 tons full displacement; 273.55 ft (84 m) overall length; 32.85 ft (10.3 m) maximum beam. **Crew:** 90.
Propulsion: 1 General Electric LM2500 gas turbine (27,400 shp) or 1 MTU 20V-956 diesel (4,800 bhp); CODOG; 2 propellers.
Sensors: 1 Plessey AWS5 search radar; 1 Philips (Sweden) 9LV200 fire control radar; 1 B&W Scanter navigational radar; 2 Raytheon EX-77 fire control radars; 1 Plessey PMS-26 hull-mounted sonar; DATA-SAAB automated action information data processor.
Armament: 2 quadruple Harpoon anti-ship missile launchers; 1 OTO-Melara 76 mm dual-purpose gun; single octuple Sea Sparrow short-range air defence missile launcher.
Top speed: 28 knots. **Range:** 2,500 nautical miles at 18 knots.
Programme: These 3 YARD of Glasgow designed KV72 corvettes were ordered in 1975. The lead ship, *Niels Juel* (F354), was laid down in October 1976, launched in September 1978 and commissioned into service in August 1980. Both laid down during 1977, the other 2 of the class, *Olfert Fischer* (F355) and *Peter Tordenskjold* (F356), were commissioned simultaneously on 7 September 1981.
Notes: Built to operate and fight in very rough water conditions these Niels Juel class vessels have provision to accept internally launched anti-submarine torpedoes and to mount the General Dynamics RAM point air defence missile system.

D'Estienne D'Orves class   Corvettes

The lead of class D'Estienne D'Orves *(F781).*

Role: Anti-submarine.   **Builder:** DCAN Lorient, France.
Users: French and Argentinian Navies.
Basic data: 1,250 tons full displacement; 262.5 ft (80 m) overall
length; 33.8 ft (10.3 m) maximum beam.   **Crew:** 75.
Propulsion: 2 SEMT-Pielstick 12 PC2 diesels (total 12,000 bhp); 2
controllable-pitch propellers.
Sensors: 1 DRBV 51 search radar; 1 DRBC 32 fire control radar; 1 Decca
1228 (DBBN 32) navigational radar; 1 DUBA 25 sonar (Diodin
in Argentinian vessels).
Armament: 2 Exocet anti-ship missile launchers; 1 single 100 mm
Model 1968 dual-purpose gun; 1 sextuple Bofors 375 mm anti-
submarine rocket launcher (1 Bofors 40 mm anti-aircraft gun on
Argentinian ships only); 1 twin Oerlikon 20 mm anti-aircraft gun;
2 triple lightweight anti-submarine torpedo tubes.
Top speed: 23.5 knots.   **Range:** 4,500 nautical miles at 15 knots.
Programme: Originally envisaged as a 14 ship class, 20 of these
vessels were in service or nearing completion by mid-1983, with 17
ordered for the French Navy and 3 in service with Argentina. Ordered
between 1972 and 1980, the French Navy class, also known as the
A69 (A signifying Aviso, or corvette) comprises: *D'Estienne D'Orves*
(F781), *Amyot d'Inville* (F782), *Drogou* (F783), *Détroyat* (F784), *Jean
Moulin* (F785), *Quartier-Maître Anquiel* (F786), *Commandant de
Pimodan* (F787), *Second Maitre Le Bihan* (F788), *Lieutenant de Vais-
seau Le Henaff* (F789), *Lieutenant de Vaisseau Lavallee* (F790), *Com-
mandant l'Herminier* (F791), *Premier Maitre l'Her* (F792),
Commandant Blaison (F793), *Enseigne de Vaisseau Jacoubet* (F794),
Commandant Ducuing (F795), *Commandant Birot* (F796) and *Com-
mandant Bouan* (F797). All of these corvettes were laid down between
September 1972 and October 1981 and all have entered service by

mid-1984. The 3 Argentinian vessels comprise: *Drummond* (F701), *Guerrico* (F702) and *Granville* (F703). Known as Drummond class ships in Argentinian service, all 3 vessels entered service between October 1978 and June 1981.

Notes: Although designed primarily for anti-submarine escort work, these corvettes carry a useful anti-ship weapons fit. Low profiled warships, these Type A69 vessels were designed to be rugged, seaworthy ships, specifically pitched at being economic on fuel and with good overall endurance, rather than high dash speed-capable ships.

D'Estienne D'Orves (*F781*) *with her midships Exocet launcher and elevated Bofors 375 mm rocket launcher clearly visible.*

Parchim class   Corvettes

The East German Navy's Parchim class bears a strong resemblance to a scaled-down Soviet-developed Koni class frigate.

Role: Anti-submarine.   **Builder:** Peenewerft, East Germany.
User: East German Navy.
Basic data: 1,200 tons full displacement; 237.9 ft (72.5 m) overall length; 30.8 ft (9.4 m) maximum beam.   **Crew:** 60.
Propulsion: 2 diesels (total 12,000 bhp); 2 propellers.
Sensors: 1 air search radar; 1 sea search and navigational radar; 1 IFF radar; 1 fire control radar (57 mm guns); 1 hull-mounted sonar.
Armament: 1 twin 57 mm and 1 twin 30 mm anti-aircraft guns; 2 quadruple SA-N-5 point air defence missile launchers; 4 medium weight anti-submarine torpedo tubes; 2 twelve-barrelled 250 mm RBU-6000 anti-submarine rocket launchers; 2 depth charge racks for 24 depth charges; mines.
Top speed: 25 knots.   **Endurance:** Over 2,000 nautical miles.
Programme: The lead of class *Parchim* (FL17) is reported to have entered service during April 1981, at which time a second vessel, *FL 45*, was nearing or had completed sea trials. Western intelligence reports indicate that up to 12 Parchim class corvettes could be constructed to supplement and ultimately replace the earlier Hai class anti-submarine corvettes operated by the East German navy.
Notes: Although smaller and lighter than the Soviet's Koni class frigate, the two vessels resemble each other closely in general outline.

Grisha I/II/III classes

Corvettes

A Soviet Navy's Grisha III coastal anti-submarine corvette.

Role: Anti-submarine.   **Builder:** Unidentified, USSR.
User: Soviet Navy.
Basic data: 1,200 tons full displacement; 239.5 ft (73.0 m) overall length; 31.8 ft (9.7 m) maximum beam.   **Crew:** 60.
Propulsion: 1 gas turbine (15,000 shp) and 4 diesels (total 16,000 bhp); CODAG; 3 propellers.
Sensors: 1 long range air search radar; 1 sea search and navigational radar; 1 fire control radar for SA-N-4 missiles (Grisha I and III only); 1 fire control radar for 57 mm guns; 1 fire control radar for 30 mm gun (Grisha III only); 1 hull-mounted and 1 dipping sonars.
Armament: 1 twin SA-N-4 short range air defence missile launcher (Grisha I and III only); 1 twin 57 mm dual-purpose gun; 1 six-barrelled 30 mm Gatling type close-in weapons system (Grisha III only); 2 twelve-barrelled 250 mm RBU-6000 anti-submarine rocket launchers; 2 twin heavyweight anti-submarine torpedo tubes; 2 depth charge racks.
Top speed: 34 knots.   **Range:** 450 nautical miles at 30 knots.
Programme: The first of 16 Grisha Is entered service in 1968, with deliveries continuing into 1974. These vessels were followed by 7 Grisha IIs, delivered between 1974 and 1976. The first of more than 34 Grisha IIIs entered service during 1975 and construction of this sub-class was reported to be continuing as of mid-1985.
Notes: Light and fast, these vessels can and frequently do operate beyond Soviet coastal waters to provide an outer surface anti-submarine screen for Soviet Navy squadrons.

Nanuchka I/II/III classes · Corvettes

A Nanuchka I of the Soviet Navy.

Role: Anti-shipping.
Users: Soviet and Indian Navies.
Builder: Petrovskiy, USSR.
Basic data: 950 tons full displacement; 229 ft (69.8 m) overall length; 40 ft (12.2 m) maximum beam.
Crew: 60.
Propulsion: 6 diesels (total 30,000 bhp); 3 propellers.
Sensors: 1 air search radar; 1 surface search and navigational radar; 1 IFF; 3 separate fire control radar systems.
Armament: 2 triple SS-N-9 anti-ship missile launchers; 1 twin SA-N-4 point air defence missile launcher; 1 twin 57 mm anti-aircraft guns in Nanuchka I and IIs, or 1 single 76 mm and 1 single 30 mm close-in weapon on Nanuchka IIIs. Export Nanuchka IIs carry only 4 SS-N-2C Styx missiles.
Top speed: 34 knots.   **Range:** 4,500 nautical miles at 15 knots.
Programme: Building of the Nanuchka class commenced in 1968, leading to the construction of a known 18 Nanuchka Is, delivered between 1969 and 1976. This phase of the programme was followed by the delivery of 3 Nanuchka IIs to the Indian Navy, comprising: *Vijaydurg* (K71), *Sindhurdurg* (K72) and *Hosdurg* (K73) between 1976 and 1978. The first of a known 4 Nanuchka IIIs were delivered to the Soviet Navy commencing in 1977.
Notes: Broad-beamed vessels, the Nanuchka class craft were designed for greater endurance and improved sea-keeping qualities when compared with earlier generation Soviet missile boats, such as the Osa class. Besides the weapons fit, which varies between the 3 sub-classes, the major difference between the Nanuchka Is and IIs, compared with the later III series, lies in the IIIs having a taller bridge structure with the large radome now above it rather than immediately aft and just forward of the mainmast.

Badr (PCG612) class
Corvettes

Badr (*PCG612*) *lead ship of the Royal Saudi Arabian Navy class.*

Role: Anti-shipping.
User: Royal Saudi Arabian Navy.
Builder: Tacoma Boat, USA.

Basic data: 815 tons full displacement; 245.0 ft (74.7 m) overall length; 31.5 ft (9.6 m) maximum beam. **Crew:** 53.

Propulsion: 1 General Electric LM2500 gas turbine (23,000 shp); 2 MTU 12V652 diesels (total 3,058 bhp); CODOG: 2 controllable-pitch propellers.

Sensors: 1 SPS-40B air search radar; 1 SPS-55 sea search and navigational radar; 1 Mk 92 fire control radar for 76 mm gun; 1 SQS-56 hull mounted sonar; automated action information data processing system.

Armament: 8 Harpoon anti-ship missile launchers; 1 single 76 mm Mk 75 (OTO-Melara) compact dual-purpose gun; 1 Phalanx 20 mm close-in weapons system; 2 single 20 mm anti-aircraft guns; 1 single 81 mm mortar; 2 single 40 mm mortars; 2 triple 324 mm torpedo tubes.

Top speed: 30 knots.   **Range:** Over 500 nautical miles at 28 knots.

Programme: This 4 ship class was ordered by Saudi Arabia in August 1977 and comprises: *Badr* (PCG612), *Al Yarmook* (PCG614), *Hitten* (PCG616) and *Tabuk* (PCG618). All laid down between May 1979 and September 1980, the ships were accepted into service between September 1981 and December 1982.

Notes: Much larger vessels than either the Ashville class or the Patrol Ship, Multi-Mission (PSMM) designs by Tacoma. In terms of defensive capability, the ships' 3-tier anti-air guns ought to prove effective even against incoming sea-skimming missiles. The 3 mortars with which the ships are equipped are intended to be used primarily for ship-to-shore bombardment. The 4 Badr class corvettes served as the flagships of the fast growing Royal Saudi Arabian Navy until delivery of the first of the French designed and built Madina class missile frigates.

Turunmaa class   Corvettes

Finland's Turunmaa (*F03*).

Role: General purpose.   **Builder:** Wartsila, Finland.
User: Finnish Naval Forces.
Basic data: 770 tons full displacement; 243.1 ft (74.1 m) overall
length; 25.6 ft (7.8 m) maximum beam.   **Crew:** 70.
Propulsion: 1 Rolls-Royce TM3B Olympus gas turbine (derated to
22,000 shp) or 3 MTU diesels (total 8,790 bhp); CODOG; 3 propellers.
Sensors: 1 Decca 1226 sea search and navigational radar; 1 Hollandse
WM 22 combined air/sea fire control radar and automated action
information data processing system.
Armament: 1 Bofors 120 mm automatic dual-purpose gun; 2 single
Bofors 40 mm anti-aircraft guns; 1 twin 23 mm anti-aircraft gun; 2
RBU-1200 five-barrel 250 mm anti-submarine rocket launchers
(internally-mounted behind amidships main-deck doors); 2 depth
charge racks.
Top speed: 35 knots.   **Range:** 2,500 nautical miles at 14 knots.
Programme: The 2 ship Turunmaa class were both laid down in
March 1967. The *Turunmaa* (F03) and *Karjala* (F04) entered service
in August and October of 1968, respectively. F03 modernised in 1985,
followed by F04 during 1986.
Notes: Long, low-profiled, angular boats, the Turunmaa class's
120 mm primary armament can fire up to 80 rounds per minute and
elevate its barrel up to angles of 80 degrees. The gun can fire at surface
targets out to an effective maximum range of around 9.7 nautical miles
(18 km). The ships have a well-balanced anti-ship, anti-air and anti-
submarine capability.

Esmeraldas class

Corvettes

Esmeraldas (*CM11*), *lead of class, seen during sea trials.*

Role: General purpose.
Users: Navies of Ecuador and Iraq.
Basic data: 700 tons full displacement; 204.4 ft (62.3 m) overall length; 30.5 ft (9.3 m) maximum beam.
Builder: CNR, Italy.
Crew: 62.
Propulsion: 4 MTU 20V956 TB92 diesels (total 24,400 bhp); 4 propellers.
Sensors: 1 Selenia/SMA RAN-10S air/sea search radar; 1 Decca TM1226 navigational radar; 1 Selenia/Elsag Orion 20X fire control radar for Albatros missile system; 1 Thomson-CSF Diodon hull-mounted sonar; Selenia IPN-10 automated action information data processing system.
Armament: Helipad for Agusta-Bell AB-212 ASW helicopter; 6 Exocet anti-ship missile launchers; 1 single 76 mm OTO-Melara compact dual-purpose gun; 1 twin Breda/Bofors rapid fire anti-aircraft gun; 2 triple 324 mm torpedo tubes.
Top speed: 38 knots. **Range:** Over 4,000 nautical miles at 18 knots.
Programme: A total of 8 of this class had been ordered by the end of 1985, consisting of 6 for Ecuador and 2 for Iraq. Ordered in 1978, the Ecuadorian vessels comprise: *Esmeraldas* (CM11), *Manabi* (CM12), *Los Ríos* (CM13), *El Oro* (CM14), *Galápagos* (CM15) and *Luja* (CM16). All were laid down between September 1979 and February 1981, with *Esmeraldas* being handed over to the Ecuadorian Navy in July 1982, with all of class delivered by May 1984. The 2 Iraqi ships of this class, *Mussa El Hassar* and *Tariq Ibn Ziad*, were ordered in early 1981 along with a later order for 4 non-helicopter-carrying corvettes from the same builder, comprising *Abdula Ibn Abiserh*, *Kalid Ibn Alwaldi*, *Saad Ibn Abi Waqqas* and *Salah Aldin Alayoobi*.
Notes: The Esmeraldas class is a development of CNR's Wadi class corvette.

Wadi class   Corvettes

The lead of class Libyan Navy vessel during 1979 sea trials.

Role: General purpose.   **Builder:** CNR Riva Trigoso, Italy.
User: Libyan Navy.
Basic data: 650 tons full displacement; 202.4 ft (61.7 m) overall length; 30.5 ft (9.3 m) maximum beam.   **Crew:** 58.
Propulsion: 4 MTU 16V956 TB91 diesels (total 16,400 bhp); 4 controllable-pitch propellers.
Sensors: 1 Selenia RAN 11 L/X combined low-level air/sea search radar; 1 Decca TM1226 sea search and navigational radar; 1 ELSAG NA 10/2 fire control radar and optronic director; Selenia IPN 10 automated action information data processing; 1 Thomson-CSF Dioden hull-mounted sonar.
Armament: 4 Otomat Mk 1 anti-ship missile launchers; 1 single 76 mm OTO-Melara Compact dual-purpose gun; 1 twin 35 mm Breda/Oerlikon anti-aircraft gun; 2 triple ILAS 3 lightweight anti-submarine torpedo tubes; 2 mine rails for up to 16 mines.
Top speed: 34 knots.   **Range:** 4,000 nautical miles at 18 knots.
Programme: Ordered in 1974, this 4 ship class comprises: *Assad Al Tadjer* (FL412), *Assad Al Tougour* (FL413), *Assad Al Khali* (FL414) and *Assad Al Hudud* (FL415). Launch dates for the 4 corvettes spanned the period between the end of April 1977 and June 1979, the vessels entering service in September 1979, February 1980, along with the simultaneous acceptance of the latter two at the close of March 1981.
Notes: This class served as the precursors of the slightly larger and much better armed and helicopter-carrying Esmeraldas class corvettes.

Pauk class

Corvettes

A Pauk class corvette of the Soviet Navy at speed, 1981.

Role: Anti-submarine.　　　　**Builder:** As yet unidentified, USSR.
User: Soviet Navy.
Basic data: 600 tons full displacement; 191.9 ft (58.5 m) overall length; 34.4 ft (10.5 m) maximum beam.　　　　**Crew:** 40.
Propulsion: 2 diesels (total 20,000 bhp); 2 propellers.
Sensors: 1 combined air/sea search radar; 1 sea search and navigational radar; 1 fire control radar (for both 76.2 and 30 mm guns); 1 each hull-mounted and stern-mounted dipping sonars; automated naval tactical information processing system.
Armament: 1 single 76.2 mm dual-purpose gun; 1 quintuple SA-N-5 Grail point air defence missile launcher; 1 multi-barrel 30 mm Gatling type close-in weapons system; 2 quintuple 250 mm anti-submarine rocket launchers; 4 medium weight anti-submarine torpedo tubes; 2 depth charge racks for 12 depth charges.
Top speed: 35 knots.　　　　**Endurance:** Over 3,000 nautical miles.
Programme: 12 of this class were known to exist by the end of 1984; the vessels being first deployed during 1980. This class could be built in large numbers, if, as seems probable, these ships have been developed as a replacement for the Soviet Navy's now ageing 62-vessel Poti class anti-submarine corvettes built in the 1960s.
Notes: The Pauk class is equipped within a dipping sonar system that is installed inside a sizeable housing standing on and extending aft of the vessel's stern.

SFCN PR 72 class   Corvettes

The Peruvian Navy's Herrera (P104), as P24 during trials.

Role: Anti-shipping.
Builders: DCAN Lorient and SFCN, France.   **User:** Peruvian Navy.
Basic data: 590 tons full displacement; 210.0 ft (64.0 m) overall
length; 29.5 ft (9.0 m) maximum beam.   **Crew:** 36.
Propulsion: 4 SACM AGO 240 diesels (total 22,000 bhp); 4 propel-
lers.
Sensors: 1 Thomson-CSF Triton combined air/sea search radar; 1
Decca TM1226 sea search and navigational radar; 1 Thomson-CSF
Castor fire control radar/optronics system; 1 IFF radar.
Armament: 4 MM38 Exocet anti-ship missile launchers; 1 single
76 mm OTO-Melara compact dual-purpose gun; 1 twin 40 mm Breda/
Bofors L40/70 anti-aircraft gun; 2 single 20 mm anti-aircraft guns; 2
heavyweight torpedo tubes.
Top speed: 38 knots.   **Range:** 2,800 nautical miles at 16 knots.
Programme: Peru placed the order for this 6-vessel class in 1978, the
ships comprising: *Velarde* (P101), *Santillana* (P102), *De los Heroes*
(P103), *Herrera* (P104), *Larrea* (P105) and *Sanchez Carrion* (P106).
The lead craft, along with the 3rd and 5th examples, were built by
DCAN Lorient, while SFCN constructed the 2nd, 4th and 6th vessels.
All launched between September 1978 and June 1979, the 6 craft
entered service between July 1980 and September 1981. A slightly
smaller PR72 MS has been supplied to Senegal and is dealt with
separately within the fast attack craft section.
Notes: Designed for all-weather, long range, ocean-going patrol, this
class employs a steel hull and light alloy superstructure.

Poti class

A Soviet Navy coastal submarine-chasing Poti class vessel.

Role: Anti-submarine. **Builders:** Various, USSR.
Users: Navies of USSR, Bulgaria and Romania.
Basic data: 580 tons full displacement; 200.1 ft (61.0 m) overall length; 25.9 ft (7.9 m) maximum beam. **Crew:** 46.
Propulsion: 2 gas turbines (total 40,000 shp) and 2 M503A diesels (total 8,000 bhp); CODAG; 2 propellers.
Sensors: 1 long range air search radar; 1 sea search and navigational radar; 1 gun fire control radar; 1 IFF radar; 1 dipping sonar.
Armament: 1 twin 57 mm anti-aircraft gun; 2 twelve-barrelled 250 mm RBU-6000 anti-submarine rocket launchers; 4 medium anti-submarine torpedo tubes.
Top speed: 36 knots. **Range:** 320 nautical miles at 32 knots.
Programme: 68 of this class are believed to have been built between 1961 and 1967. Although considered obsolete, at least 40 of these vessels were reported to be in service with the Soviet Navy's coastal forces in mid-1983, at which time 3 each of this class served with the navies of Bulgaria and Romania.
Notes: Classified as Malyy Protivolodochnyy Korabl', or small anti-submarine ships by the Soviet Navy, the Poti class and their heirs apparent in the shape of the Pauk class have no real equivalent in service with the major Western world navies and, as such, help to highlight the Soviet Navy's doctrine of, where applicable, opting to go for quantity rather than quality.

Lurssen FPB 57 classes   Fast attack craft

The Nigerian Navy's Damisa *(P179) at speed, 1980.*

Role: Anti-shipping.

Builders: Lurssen, Federal Germany and Turkish Naval Dockyards.

Users: Navies of Turkey (6), Nigeria (3) and Kuwait (2).

Basic data: 444 tons full displacement; 190.6 ft (58.1 m) overall length; 25.0 ft (7.62 m) maximum beam.   **Crew:** 54.

Propulsion: 4 MTU 16V956 TB91 diesels (total 19,940 bhp); 4 propellers.

Sensors: 1 Decca 1226 sea search and navigational radar; 1 Hollandse WM28 fire control radar and automated action information data processing system.

Armament: 8 Harpoon (Turkish craft) or 4 Otomat Mk 2 (Nigerian craft) or 4MM 40 Exocet (Kuwaiti craft) anti-ship missile launchers; 1 single 76 mm OTO-Melara compact dual-purpose gun; 1 twin 40 mm Breda/Bofors anti-aircraft gun or 1 twin 35 mm Oerlikon anti-aircraft gun (Kuwaiti craft); 2 single 7.62 mm machine guns.

Top speed: 40 knots.   **Range:** 2,000 nautical miles at 16 knots.

Programme: A total of 11 of these craft had been ordered by mid-1985, all of which had been completed. The initial contract came from Turkey in August 1973; with Lurssen to build the lead boat, *P340* while the rest, *P341* through *P345*, were to be constructed in Turkey. The next contract, for 3 craft came from Nigeria, whose *P178* through *P180* had all been delivered by April 1981. The Kuwaiti order for 2 craft, *K571* and *K572*, was fulfilled with deliveries being completed by mid-1983.

Notes: The FPB 57 craft use an all-steel hull structure, married to a light alloy superstructure.

Type 143/143A classes

Fast attack craft

The Federal German Navy's second of Type 143, Falke (P6112).

Role: Anti-shipping.
Builders: Lurssen and Kroger, Federal Germany.
User: Federal German Navy (10 × T143 and 10 × T143A).
Basic data: 393 tons full displacement; 189.0 ft (57.6 m) overall length; 25.5 ft (7.76 m) maximum beam.
Crew: 39 (143); 34 (143A).
Propulsion: 4 MTU 16V956 TB91 diesels (total 16,000 bhp); 4 propellers.
Sensors: 1 SMA 3RM 20 sea search and navigational radar; 1 Hollandse WM 27 fire control radar; AGIS automated action information data processing system.
Armament: 4MM 38 Exocet anti-ship missile launchers; 2 single 76 mm OTO-Melara Compact dual-purpose guns on Type 143s or aft mount replaced on Type 143As by a single 24-cell General Dynamics RAM point air defence missile launcher when available; 2 single 533 mm torpedo tubes (Type 143 only); mines.
Top speed: 36 knots.   **Range:** 2,000 nautical miles at 16 knots.
Programme: These classes consist of 10 craft each for a total of 20 vessels. The Type 143s comprise: P6111/S61 through P6120/S70; all entering service between April 1976 and December 1977. The Type 143As comprise: P6121/S71 through P6130/S80, all delivered between late 1982 and late 1984. Lurssen acted as lead yard for the ships, 3 of each class being constructed under sub-contract by Kroger.
Notes: The Type 143 and 143A craft employ a steel-framed hull sheathed with wood planking married to a light alloy superstructure.

PGG511/As Siddiq class

Fast attack craft

As Siddiq (*PGG511*), *lead of this nine vessel class.*

Role: Anti-shipping.　　　　　　**Builder:** Peterson Builders, USA.
User: Royal Saudi Arabian Navy.
Basic data: 390 tons full displacement; 190.0 ft (57.9 m) overall length; 26.5 ft (8.1 m) maximum beam.　　　　　**Crew:** 38.
Propulsion: 1 General Electric LM2500 gas turbine (23,000 shp); 2 MTU 12V652 diesels (total 3,058 bhp); CODOG; 2 controllable-pitch propellers.
Sensors: 1 SPS-55 sea search and navigational radar; 1 Mk 92 fire control radar for 76 mm gun.
Armament: 4 Harpoon anti-ship missile launchers; 1 single 76 mm Mk 75 (OTO-Melara) compact dual-purpose gun; 1 Phalanx 20 mm close-in weapons system; 2 single 20 mm anti-aircraft guns; 1 single 81 mm mortar; 2 single 40 mm mortars.
Top speed: 38 knots.　　**Range:** Over 500 nautical miles at 32 knots.
Programme: Saudi Arabia ordered this 9 ship class in February 1977, the vessels comprising; *As Siddiq* (PGG511), *Al Farouq* (PGG513), *Abdul Aziz* (PGG515), *Faisal* (PGG517), *Khalid* (PGG519), *Amr* (PGG521), *Tariq* (PGG523), *Oqbah* (PGG525) and *Abu Obaidah* (PGG527). All delivered between December 1980 to December 1982.
Notes: The large funnel is necessitated by the air intake and exhaust needs of the gas turbine.

Province class

Fast attack craft

SNV Dhofar (*B10*), *operated by Oman, 1982.*

Role: Anti-shipping.   **Builder:** Vosper Thornycroft, UK.
Users: Omani Navy (4), Kenyan Navy (2).
Basic data: 370 tons full displacement; 186 ft (56.7 m) overall length;
26.9 ft (8.2 m) maximum beam.   **Crew:** 65.
Propulsion: 4 Paxman Valenta 18GM diesels (total 15,200 bhp); 4
propellers.
Sensors: 1 Decca AC 1226 sea search and navigational radar; 1
Sperry Sea Archer optronic fire control system; IFF facilities.
Armament: 4 Exocet (or 8 Sea Killer optional fit) anti-ship missile
launchers; 1 single 76 mm OTO-Melara compact dual-purpose gun; 1
twin Breda/Bofors 40 mm anti-aircraft gun.
Top speed: 38 knots.   **Range:** 2,000 nautical miles at 16 knots.
Programme: The first of this 3 craft class was ordered late in 1979,
to be followed by a further 2 craft order in January 1981. The class
comprises SNV *Dhofar* (B10), *Al Bat'Nar* (B11) and *Al Sharqiyah*
(B12). All three were laid down between September 1980 and December 1981 and were completed in July 1982, November 1983 and January 1984 respectively; 2 additional craft of the same basic design,
reportedly for Kenya, were in build by early 1985, followed by an order
for a fourth Omani craft placed in January 1986.
Notes: The total cost of the 3 craft Omani programme was put at
around £75 million in 1981 values.

Stockholm class   Fast attack craft

Stockholm (*K11*) *with missiles yet to be fitted.*

Role: Anti-shipping.   **Builder:** Karlskronavarvet, Sweden.
User: Royal Swedish Navy.
Basic data: 300 tons full displacement; 164.0 ft (50.0 m) overall
length; 24.6 ft (7.5 m) maximum beam.   **Crew:** 26.
Propulsion: 1 Allison 570-KF gas turbine (15,000 shp) and 2 MTU
16V396 diesels (total 7,200 bhp); CODAG; 2 controllable-pitch pro-
pellers.
Sensors: 1 Ericson Sea Giraffe pulse doppler air search radar: 1 Racal
Decca 1229 sea search and navigational radar; 1 Philips (Sweden)
9LV200 fire control radar and automated action information data pro-
cessing system.
Armament: 6 SAAB-Bofors RBS 15 anti-ship missile launchers; 1
single 57 mm SAK 57 Mk 2 compact dual-purpose gun; 1 single 40 mm
Bofors L 40/70 anti-aircraft gun; 2 single heavyweight anti-submarine
torpedo tubes.
Top speed: 38 knots.   **Range:** 2,000 nautical miles at 18 knots.
Programme: The first 2 of this 6 craft class were ordered by the
Swedish Government in September 1981. The lead of class, *Stockholm*
(K11) was laid down in August 1982, followed by *Malmo* (K12) in
March 1983. Initial deployment of this class occurred in March 1985
with the commissioning of *Stockholm.*
Notes: The Stockholm class carries a heavy and well balanced arma-
ment, backed by effective sensors.

Helsinki class

Fast attack craft

Helsinki (*P60*), *the lead craft of this Finnish class in mid-1983, as yet to be equipped with its four Swedish-developed anti-ship missiles.*

Role: Anti-shipping. **Builder:** Wartsila, Finland.
User: Finnish Defence Force.
Basic data: 300 tons full displacement; 147.6 ft (45.0 m) overall length; 29.2 ft (8.9 m) maximum beam. **Crew:** 30.
Propulsion: 3 MTU 16V 538 diesels (total 12,000 bhp); 3 controllable-pitch propellers.
Sensors: 1 combined low-level air/sea search radar; 1 navigational radar; 1 Philips (Sweden) 9LV225 electro-optronic fire control and automated action information processing system.
Armament: 4 SAAB RBS 15 anti-ship missile launchers; 1 single 57 mm Bofors SAK-57 Mk 1 dual-purpose gun; 2 single 23 mm anti-aircraft guns
Top speed: 33 knots. **Endurance:** In excess of 2,000 nautical miles.
Programme: The first of this planned 8 craft class was ordered in October 1978, launched in September 1980 and delivered to the Finnish Defence Force in January 1981. This prototype vessel, *Helsinki* (P60) has now been joined by *Turkhu* (P61) and *Oulu* (P62), with *P63* in build.
Notes: This Finnish-designed fast attack craft class breaks with convention in terms of its hull proportions, being much broader of beam in relation to its length than any of its contemporaries from the drawing boards of Lurssen or Vosper Thornycroft.

Racharit class   Fast attack craft

Thailand's Racharit *(4)*, *lead craft of a 3 vessel class.*

Role: Anti-shipping.   **Builder:** C.N. Breda, Italy.
User: Thai Navy.
Basic data: 270 tons full displacement; 163.4 ft (49.8 m) overall
length; 24.6 ft (7.5 m) maximum beam.   **Crew:** 45.
Propulsion: 3 MTU 20V538 TB91 diesels (total 13,500 bhp); 3
controllable-pitch propellers.
Sensors: 1 Decca TM1226 sea search/navigational radar; 1 Hollandse
M25 fire control radar.
Armament: 4 Exocet anti-ship missile launchers; 1 single 76 mm
OTO-Melara compact dual-purpose gun; 1 single 40 mm Breda/Bofors
anti-aircraft gun.
Top speed: 36 knots.   **Range:** 2,000 nautical miles at 15 knots.
Programme: Thailand ordered this 3 craft class in July 1976, the
vessels comprising: *Racharit* (4), *Witthayakom* (5) and *Udomet* (6).
All launched between July and September of 1978, the 3 respectively
entered service in August 1979, November 1979 and February 1980.
Notes: A sturdy looking design in many ways directly comparable to
the near contemporary, if heavier Vosper Thornycroft-developed Ramadan class. While the Racharits appear to haul the same kind of
sensor/weapons fit over similar range at comparable speeds, all on the
power of 3 rather than 4 diesels, the lower crew complement of the
Ramadan class suggests a higher degree of automation has been designed into the latter.

Matka class   Fast attack craft

This Matka class craft is seen accelerating towards foilborne cruise.

Role: Anti-shipping.   **Builder:** Izhora Shipyard, USSR.
User: Soviet Navy.
Basic data: 260 tons full displacement; 131.2 ft (40.0 m) overall
length; 25.25 ft (7.7 m) maximum beam of hull.   **Crew:** 30.
Propulsion: 3 M504 diesels (total 15,000 bhp); 3 propellers.
Sensors: 1 combined low-level air/sea search and navigational radar;
1 fire control radar (for SS-N-2C missiles); 1 fire control radar (for
76.2 mm and 30 mm guns); 2 separate IFF radars; naval tactical infor-
mation processing system.
Armament: 2 single SS-N-2C anti-ship missile launchers; 1 single
76.2 mm dual-purpose gun; 1 multi-barrel 30 mm Gatling type close-
in weapons system.
Top speed: 40 knots.   **Range:** 400 nautical miles at 36 knots.
Programme: A known 16 craft class, this hydrofoil was reported to
have initially deployed with the Soviet Fleet during 1978.
Notes: The Matka class design is a missile equipped derivative of the
Soviet Navy's Turya class torpedo-carrying hydrofoil. Judging from the
Matka craft's relatively modest performance and weapons carrying
capability, compared with the much lighter Sparviero class hydrofoil,
it would appear that the Matka design is less than adequately powered
for its task.

Lurssen TNC 45 classes   Fast attack craft

Abu Dhabi's Baniyas (*P4501*), *seen on contractor's trials.*

Role: Anti-shipping.   **Builder:** Lurssen, Federal Germany.
Users: Navies of Argentina (2), Bahrain (2) and Kuwait (6).
Basic data: 259 tons full displacement; 147.3 ft (44.9 m) overall
length; 23.0 ft (7.0 m) maximum beam.   **Crew:** 33.
Propulsion: 4 MTU 16V538 TB92 diesels (total 15,600 bhp); 4 pro-
pellers.
Sensors: 1 Philips (Sweden) 9LV223 fire control radar and automated
action information data processing system; 1 IFF Mk 10 radar; CSEE
Panda optical fire director.
Armament: 2 twin MM40 Exocet anti-ship missile launchers; 1 single
76 mm OTO-Melara compact dual-purpose gun; 1 single 40 mm
Breda/Bofors L 70B anti-aircraft gun; 2 single MG-3 machine guns.
Top speed: 41.5 knots.   **Range:** 1,500 nautical miles at 16 knots.
Programme: Argentina was the first customer for this export version
of the Lurssen-developed Federal German Navy's Type 148, placing a
contract for 2 craft, *Intrépida* (ELPR1) and *Indómita* (ELPR2) in 1974;
the vessels being delivered in July and December 1975. Subsequently, both Bahrain and Kuwait ordered 2 and 6 craft, respectively;
the 2 Bahrain vessels being scheduled for 1982 and 1983 delivery,
while Kuwaiti deliveries commenced in late 1982.
Notes: Steel-hulled with aluminium superstructures, the TNC in the
designation is an abbreviation of Top speed Navy Craft.

Rade Koncar class
Fast attack craft

The lead of class, Rade Koncar *(PGG401), of the Yugoslavian Navy at speed. Powered by British gas turbines and German diesels, these craft are armed with Soviet missiles and Swedish guns.*

Role: Anti-shipping.   **Builder:** Tito Shipyards, Yugoslavia.
Users: Navies of Yugoslavia and Libya.
Basic data: 250 tons full displacement; 147.6 ft (45.0 m) overall length; 26.2 ft (8.0 m) maximum beam.   **Crew:** 30.
Propulsion: 2 Rolls-Royce Proteus gas turbines (total 9,000 shp) and 2 MTU diesels (total 7,200 bhp); CODAG; 4 controllable-pitch propellers.
Sensors: 1 Philips (Sweden) 9LV 200 missile and gun fire control radar system, 1 IFF; 1 Decca 1226 sea search and navigational radar; Philips (Sweden) automated action data processing system.
Armament: 2 single SS-N-2B Styx anti-ship missile launchers; 2 single 57 mm Bofors D70 dual-purpose guns.
Top speed: 37 knots.   **Range:** 1,650 nautical miles at 15 knots.
Programme: This 6 craft class comprises; *Rade Koncar* (PGG401), *Vlado Cetkovic* (402), *Ramiz Sadiku* (403), *Hasan Zahirovic Lase* (404), *Jordan Nikolov Orce* (405) and *Ante Banina* (406). All entered service between April 1977 and December 1979. Libya ordered 4 of this class in early 1985.
Notes: This extremely compact Yugoslavian designed craft carries an interesting weapons balance of missiles and high capability guns.

Ashville class　　　　　　　　　　　　**Fast attack craft**

The former USS Grand Rapids *(PG98) at speed*.

Role: Anti-shipping.
Builders: Tacoma Boat and Peterson Builders, USA.
Users: Navies of Colombia (2), South Korea (1) and Turkey (2).
Basic data: 245 tons full displacement; 164.5 ft (50.1 m) overall length; 23.9 ft (7.3 m) maximum beam.　　　　　　**Crew:** 28.
Propulsion: 1 General Electric LM1500 gas turbine (13,300 shp); 2 Cummins VT12-S75M diesels (total 3,300 bhp); CODOG; 2 controllable-pitch propellers.
Sensors: 1 Raytheon Pathfinder combined low-level air/sea search and navigational radar; 1 SPG-50 fire control radar.
Armament: 1 single 3-inch Mk 34 anti-aircraft gun; 1 single 40 mm Mk 3 anti-aircraft gun; 2 twin 0.5 inch machine guns.
Top speed: Over 40 knots.　**Range:** 1,700 nautical miles at 16 knots.
Programme: A total of 17 craft of this class were built for the US Navy; all being delivered between 1966 and 1971. The first transfer of this class to US allied navies commenced with the delivery of *Paek Ku 51* to South Korea in October 1971; 4 more Ashvilles were transferred in pairs to Greece, which no longer operates them, and Turkey, which continues to operate *Yildirim* (P338) and *Bora* (P339). More recently, the last 2 US Navy craft, *Tacoma* and *Welch* were leased to Colombia in 1982.
Notes: The Ashville class requirement was brought into focus by the Cuban crisis of 1962 and the subsequent US Navy realisation that it lacked modern, high speed interdiction craft.

Handalan class   Fast attack craft

Handalan (*P3511*) *lead craft of the Royal Malaysian Navy class.*

Role: Anti-shipping.   **Builder:** Karlskronavarvet, Sweden.
User: Royal Malaysian Navy.
Basic data: 240 tons full displacement; 143.0 ft (43.6 m) overall length; 23.3 ft (7.1 m) maximum beam.   **Crew:** 40.
Propulsion: 3 MTU 16V538 TB91 diesels (total 10,800 bhp); 3 propellers.
Sensors: 1 Philips (Sweden) 9LV 200 combined air/sea search and tracking radar and fire control system with automated action information data processing.
Armament: 2 twin MM40 Exocet anti-ship missile launchers; 1 single 57 mm Bofors SAK57 Mk 1 dual-purpose gun; 1 single 40 mm Bofors anti-aircraft gun; provision to carry 2 heavyweight anti-submarine, wire-guided homing torpedoes.
Top speed: 34.5 knots.   **Range:** 1,850 nautical miles at 14 knots.
Programme: An 8 craft class, the first 4 of which were ordered by Malaysia in August 1976 comprising: *Handalan* (P3511), *Perkasa* (P3512), *Pendikar* (P3513) and *Gempita* (P3514). All of this first batch were laid down between May 1977 and October 1977; the 4 being accepted simultaneously in late October 1979. Malaysia placed a repeat order for a further 4 of these craft in December 1982.
Notes: The Handalan class, or Spica M design, is a more heavily anti-ship armed derivative of the Royal Swedish Navy's Spica II class craft and are the first new-built Swedish vessels to be exported in the post-World War II period.

Osa I/II classes   Fast attack craft

Yugoslavia's Osa I, Mitar Acev (*P301*).

Role: Anti-shipping.   **Builders:** Various, USSR and China.
Users: Navies of Algeria (8), Bulgaria (1), China (around 90), Cuba (13), East Germany (15), Egypt (6), Finland (4), India (8), Iraq (4), Libya (12), North Korea (8), Poland (13), Romania (5), Somalia (2), Syria (6), USSR (105) and Yugoslavia (10).
Basic data: 240 tons full displacement; 127.95 ft (39.0 m) overall length; 25.25 ft (7.7 m) maximum beam.   **Crew:** 30.
Propulsion: 3 M504 diesels (15,000 bhp); 3 propellers in Osa IIs; Osa I have 3 M503A diesels (12,000 bhp); 3 propellers.
Sensors: 1 combined low-level air/sea search and navigational radar; 1 fire control radar (for 30 mm guns); 3 separate IFF radars.
Armament: 4 single SS-N-2 Styx anti-ship missile launchers; 2 twin 30 mm Gatling type close-in weapons systems.
Top speed: 36 knots.   **Range:** 700 nautical miles at 20 knots.
Programme: The USSR built approximately 240 Osa I and IIs comprising 120 for the Soviet Navy (70 Osa Is and 50 Osa IIs), plus a known 118 for export to friendly navies (70 Osa Is and 48 Osa IIs); deliveries being completed between 1959 and 1970. In addition, approximately 90 Osa Is have been built in the Chinese People's Republic, with deliveries commencing in 1960.
Notes: With a total of around 330 Osa I and IIs built, this steel-hulled design can rightfully lay claim to being not only the largest post-World War II warship programme, but also to being the most widely used fast attack craft extant.

Norrkoping class

Fast attack class

Pitea (*R138*) equipped with Sea Giraffe search radar and missiles.

Role: Anti-shipping. **Builder:** Karlskronavarvet, Sweden.
User: Royal Swedish Navy.
Basic data: 230 tons full displacement; 143.0 ft (43.6 m) overall length; 23.3 ft (7.1 m) maximum beam. **Crew:** 27.
Propulsion: 3 Rolls-Royce Proteus gas turbines (total 12,900 shp); 3 propellers.
Sensors: 1 Scanter 009 sea search and navigational radar (to be replaced by Ericson Sea Giraffe combined air/sea and navigational radar); 1 Philips (Sweden) 9LV200 fire control radar and automated action information data processing system.
Armament: 8 RBS-15 anti-ship missile launchers (from 1984) or 6 single 533 mm torpedo tubes; 1 single 57 mm Bofors SAK 57 Mk 1 dual-purpose gun; mines.
Top speed: 40 knots. **Range:** Over 700 nautical miles at 35 knots.
Programme: This 12 craft class comprises: *Norrkoping* (R131), *Nynashamn* (R132), *Nortalje* (R133), *Varberg* (R134), *Vasteras* (R135), *Vastervik* (R136), *Umea* (R137), *Pitea* (R138), *Lulea* (R139), *Halmstad* (R140), *Stromstad* (R141) and *Ystad* (R142). All of this class entered service between September 1973 and December 1976.
Notes: The Norrkoping hull, married to an all diesel propulsion arrangement and different weapons fit, served as the basis for the Handalan class craft exported to Malaysia. This class is also often referred to as Spica II.

Lurssen FPB 38 class

Fast attack craft

The lead of this two-craft Bahraini Navy class, P10, 1981.

Role: Patrol. **Builders:** Lurssen, Federal Germany and Malaysia.
Users: Bahrain Navy (2), Federal German Coast Guard (8) and Royal
Malaysian Marine Police (12).
Basic data: 186 tons full displacement; 126.3 ft (38.5 m) overall
length; 23.0 ft (7.0 m) maximum beam. **Crew:** 21 (Bahrain).
Propulsion: 2 MTU 20V539 TB91 diesels (total 7,800 bhp); 2 pro-
pellers.
Sensors: 1 Racal Decca TM1226 sea search and navigational radar;
1 Philips (Sweden) 9LV100 fire control radar and automated action
information data processing system; 1 CSEE Lynx optical fire control
system (Bahraini craft).
Armament: 1 twin 40 mm Breda/Bofors 40 L70B anti-aircraft gun; 2
single 7.62 mm MG3 machine guns; 14 mines (Bahraini craft fit).
Top speed: 33 knots. **Range:** 1,150 nautical miles at 16 knots.
Programme: Designed as a coast guard patrol craft during the latter
half of the 1960s, Bahrain, in 1979, ordered the first 2 more powerfully
armed and sensored naval craft versions, these vessels, *P10* and *P11*,
being delivered during 1981.
Notes: Built around a standard hull design made of steel, all of the
FPB 38 vessels employ an aluminium superstructure.

Brooke Marine 37.5 m class   Fast attack craft

P342, *the second of five operated by Algeria.*

Role: Anti-shipping.   **Builder:** Brooke Marine (lead), UK.
Users: Navies of Oman (6) and Algeria (5).
Basic data: 180 tons full displacement; 123 ft (37.5 m) overall length;
20 ft (6.1 m) maximum beam.   **Crew:** 27.
Propulsion: 2 Paxman Ventura YJCM diesels (total 4,800 bhp); 2
propellers.
Sensors: 1 Decca TM916 sea search and navigational radar; 1 Sperry
Sea Archer optronic fire control system.
Armament: 2 Exocet anti-ship missile launchers (on B-2 and B-3
only); 1 single 76 mm OTO-Melara dual-purpose gun; 2 single
12.7 mm machine guns.
Top speed: 26 knots.   **Range:** 2,800 nautical miles at 12 knots.
Programme: Originally a 7 craft class comprising B-1 through B-7.
Delivered between March 1973 and August 1977, the first 3 craft were
modified to carry Exocet between 1977 and 1979, but B-1 was lost
during its return to Oman in November 1978. Algeria ordered 5 of
these craft in late 1980, comprising *P341* through *P345*, the first two
being built by Brooke Marine, while the last three were built locally in
Algeria's Mer-el-Kebir yards.
Notes: Developed from Brooke Marine's smaller 108 feet (32.9 mm)
Standard Patrol Craft.

Shershen class   Fast attack craft

Biokovak (*P221*), *the 11th of a 14 craft Yugoslavian Navy class.*

Role: Anti-shipping.
Builders: Various, USSR and Tito SY, Yugoslavia.
Users: Navies of USSR (30), Yugoslavia (14), Angola (6), Cape Verde Islands (3), Egypt (6), East Germany (18), Guinea (3), North Korea (4) and Vietnam (8).
Basic data: 160 tons full displacement; 111.5 ft (34.0 m) overall length; 23.6 ft (7.2 m) maximum beam.   **Crew:** 21.
Propulsion: 3 M503A diesels (total 12,000 bhp); 3 propellers.
Sensors: 1 combined low-level air/sea search and navigational radar; 1 fire control radar (for 30 mm guns); 2 separate IFF radars.
Armament: 4 single 533 mm torpedo tubes; 2 twin 30 mm Gatling type close-in weapons systems; 2 depth charge racks with a total of up to 12 depth charges. Note: a number of these craft, including the Cape Verde, 3 Egyptian and some East German vessels have had their torpedo tubes removed.
Top speed: 45 knots.   **Range:** 700 nautical miles at 20 knots.
Programme: Approximately 80 of this class were built in Soviet shipyards between 1963 and 1970, plus a further 10 built in Yugoslavia between 1966 and 1971.
Notes: The Shershen class has a wooden hull and was designed in parallel with the missile-carrying Osa I class. Compared with the Osa class, the Shershen design employs the same propulsive machinery married to a smaller hull, hence the latter's higher top speed.

Hugin class

Fast attack craft

Munin (*P152*), *second craft of this Royal Swedish Navy class.*

Role: Anti-shipping.
Builders: Bergens and Westermoens, Norway.
User: Royal Swedish Navy.
Basic data: 150 tons full displacement; 119.85 ft (36.53 m) overall length; 20.3 ft (6.2 m) maximum beam. **Crew:** 22.
Propulsion: 2 MTU 20V672 TB90 diesels (total 7,200 bhp); 2 propellers.
Sensors: 1 Scanter 009 sea search and navigational radar; 1 Philips (Sweden) 9LV200 Mk 2 fire control radar and automated action information data processing system; 1 Simrad SQ3D/SF hull-mounted sonar.
Armament: 6 Penguin Mk 2 anti-ship missile launchers or 24 mines or 2 depth charge racks; 1 single 57 mm Bofors SAK57 Mk 1 dual-purpose gun
Top speed: 35 knots. **Range:** 550 nautical miles at 35 knots.
Programme: Sweden ordered a prototype of this derivative of the Storm class design from Bergens in the early 1970s. This craft, *Jagaren* (P150) was delivered in 1972. A contract for a further 16 craft was placed with Bergens in 1975 for: *Hugin* (P151), *Munin* (P152), *Magne* (P153), *Mode* (P154), *Vale* (P155), *Vidar* (P156), *Mjolner* (P157), *Mysing* (P158), *Kaparen* (P159), *Vaktaren* (P160), *Snapphanen* (P161), *Spejaren* (P162), *Styrbjorn* (P163), *Starkodder* (P164), *Tordon* (P165) and *Tirfing* (P166); all entering service between July 1978 and 1982. All but P154 through P158 were built by Bergens.
Notes: Scheduled to have Penguin missiles replaced by RBS-15s.

Storm class   Fast attack craft

KNM Glint (*P962*), with a Hauk class craft beyond.

Role: Anti-shipping.
Builders: Bergens MV and Westermoen, Norway.
User: Royal Norwegian Navy.
Basic data: 125 tons full displacement; 119.8 ft (36.53 m) overall length; 20.7 ft (6.3 m) maximum beam.   **Crew:** 26.
Propulsion: 2 Maybach (MTU) MB 872A diesels (total 7,200 bhp); 2 propellers.
Sensors: 1 Decca TM1226 sea search and navigational radar; 1 Hollandse WM 26 fire control radar.
Armament: 4 or 6 Penguin anti-ship missile launchers, replaceable by 2 depth charge racks; 1 single 76 mm Bofors gun; 1 single 40 mm Bofors anti-aircraft gun.
Top speed: 37 knots.   **Range:** 550 nautical miles at 36 knots.
Programme: Originally a 20 craft class comprising: *Storm* (P960), *Blink* (P961), *Glint* (P962), *Skjold* (P963), *Trygg* (P964), *Kjekk* (P965), *Djerv* (P966), *Skudd* (P967), *Arg* (P968), *Steil* (P969), *Brann* (P970), *Tross* (P971), *Hvass* (P972), *Traust* (P973), *Brott* (P974), *Odd* (P975), *Pil* (P976), *Brask* (P977), *Rokk* (P978) and *Gnist* (P979). Bergens were responsible for the construction of P960, 961, 962, 964, 965, 967, 968, 970, 971, 973, 974, 976, 977 and 979, while Westermoen built the remainder of this class. All entered service between mid-1965 and late 1967. (Note: *Pil* (P976) is no longer in service.)
Notes: Designed in the early 1960s as gun-equipped fast patrol boats, the Storm class was modernised during the early 1970s to carry the Norwegian-developed Penguin missile.

Castle class   Patrol vessels

HMS Leeds Castle *(P258), August 1981.*

Role: Offshore protection.   **Builder:** Hall Russell, UK.
User: Royal Navy.
Basic data: 1,450 tons full displacement; 265.75 ft (81 m) overall length; 37.75 ft (11.5 m) maximum beam.   **Crew:** 50.
Propulsion: 2 Ruston 12RKCM diesels (total 5,640 bh); 2 propellers.
Sensors: 1 Kelvin Hughes Type 1006 sea search and navigational radar; 1 Decca CANE automatic plotter; 1 Kelvin Hughes Type 778A echo sounder.
Armament: Facility to operate 1 up to Sea King sized helicopter; 1 Bofors 40 mm Mk 3 gun; 2 machine guns.
Top speed: 19.5 knots.   **Range:** 10,000 nautical miles at 12 knots.
Programme: Initially known as the Offshore Protection Vessel (OPV) Mk 2, the first order for 2 Royal Navy ships was placed in August 1980. These ships, HMS *Leeds Castle* (P258) and HMS *Dumbarton Castle* (P259), are now in service, having been accepted in August 1981 and March 1982, respectively.
Notes: The Castles are the largest of a series of Hall Russell-developed OPVs to be built so far. As with the earlier Jura and Island class ships from the same yards, the Castles are built to Lloyd's Register commercial standards, rather than to costlier naval practices. The Castle class can accommodate 25 marines in addition to the crew.

Halcon class   **Patrol vessels**

Mantilla (*GC24*), *the lead of class, during 1982 sea trials.*

Role: Off-shore patrol.   **Builder:** Bazan, Spain.
Users: Argentinian coastguard and Mexican Navy.
Basic data: 910 tons full displacement; 220.0 ft (67.0 m) overall length; 34.4 ft (10.5 m) maximum beam.   **Crew:** 34.
Propulsion: 2 Bazan-built MTU MA 16V956 TB91 diesels (total 9,000 bhp); 2 propellers.
Sensors: 1 Decca AC 1226 navigational radar; 1 Kelvin Hughes MS-39 echo sounder; 1 Koden KS-508 VHF radio direction finder.
Armament: 1 Aerospatiale Alouette III helicopter; 1 single 40 mm Breda/Bofors 40L/70 anti-aircraft gun; 2 single light machine guns.
Top speed: 22 knots.   **Range:** 4,343 nautical miles at 18 knots.
Programme: The initial order for 5 ships of this class was placed by Argentina in March 1979, comprising: *Mantilla* (GC24), *Azopardo* (GC25), *Thomson* (GC26), *Prefecto Fique* (GC27) and *Prefecto Derbes* (GC28). All were delivered by 1983. A further 6 of this class were ordered for service with the Mexican Navy in November 1980, these being. *Cadete Virgilio Uribe* (GH01), *Teniente Jose Azueta* (GH02), *Capitan de Fregata Pedro Sainz de Barranda* (GH03), *Contral-mirante Castillo Breton* (GH04), *Vicealmirante Orthon P. Blanco* (GH05) and *Contralmirante Angel Ortiz Monasterio* (GH06): all of which were completed between September and December 1982.
Notes: This currently 11-ship programme is certainly impressive in industrial terms, with all vessels being completed within 45 months of receiving the first order.

Peacock class

HMS Peacock (*P239*), *1983*.

Role: Offshore patrol.
User: Royal Navy.
Builder: Hall Russell, UK.
Basic data: 710 tons full displacement; 205.4 ft (62.6 m) overall length; 32.8 ft (10.0 m) maximum beam. **Crew:** 42.
Propulsion: 2 APE Crossley Pielstick 18 PA6V280 diesels (total 14,400 bhp); 1 propeller.
Sensors: 1 Kelvin Hughes Type 1006 sea search and navigational radar; 1 Kelvin Hughes Type MS45 Mk II echo sounder; 1 Sperry Sea Archer electro-optical fire control system.
Armament: 1 single 76 mm OTO-Melara compact dual-purpose gun; 4 single machine guns.
Top speed: 25 knots. **Endurance:** 2,500 nautical miles.
Programme: A 5-ship class, ordered in July 1981, for use with the Royal Navy's Hong Kong Patrol. The class is led by HMS *Peacock* (P239), launched in December 1982. The remaining four vessels are HMS *Plover* (P240), HMS *Starling* (P241), HMS *Swallow* (P242) and HMS *Swift* (P243), the whole class being accepted between October 1983 and March 1985.
Notes: The Peacock class replace the 5 Coniston class former minesweepers used to patrol Hong Kong waters. More compact, but more heavily armed and faster than either of their Island or Castle class forebears, the Peacock class is equipped to be replenished at sea and carry 2 Avon Searider outboard-powered inflatable boarding craft.

Pedro Teixeira class

Patrol vessels

The Brazilian Navy's Raposo Tavares *(P21) with its Bell 206 Jetranger on the ship's helipad.*

Role: River patrol. **Builder:** Brazilian Naval Dockyards.
User: Brazilian Navy.
Basic data: 690 tons full displacement; 208.5 ft (63.56 m) overall length; 31.85 ft (9.71 m) maximum beam. **Crew:** 60.
Propulsion: 4 MAN V6V16/18 TLS diesels (total 3,840 bhp); 2 propellers.
Sensors: 2 Decca 1216A sea search and navigational radars; 1 TACAN aircraft homer.
Armament: 1 Bell 206 Jetranger helicopter; 1 single 40 mm Bofors anti-aircraft gun; 2 single 81 mm mortars; 6 single 12.7 mm machine guns.
Top speed: 16 knots. **Range:** 5,500 nautical miles at 10 knots.
Programme: Ordered in late 1970, this 2 ship class comprises: *Pedro Teixeira* (P20) and *Raposo Tavares* (P21). Both were launched simultaneously in early June 1972 and entered service in mid-December 1973.
Notes: Specifically designed to operate in very shallow waters and to have a high degree of slow speed manœuvrability, these vessels carry out a multiplicity of duties, including assistance to the civil population. The ships can be used as troop and equipment transports or for river policing, and each is equipped with facilities, including a hangar, with which to operate a helicopter.

Fairey Tracker class

Patrol vessels

Royal Navy Reserve's HMS Hunter (*P284*).

Role: Patrol/rescue/fast dispatch.　　**Builder:** Fairy Marine, UK.
Users: Navies of Sierra Leone (1), South Africa (2), UK (5) and
Yemen People's Republic (1), plus numerous non-naval operators.
Basic data: 34 tons full displacement; 65.6 ft (20.0 m) overall length;
17.0 ft (5.15 m) maximum beam.　　　　　　**Crew:** Up to 11.
Propulsion: 2 Rolls-Royce DV8TCWM (total 1,500 bhp) on South
African, or 2 MTU 8V331 TC82 (total 1,800 bhp) on Yemen or 2
General Motors 12V71TI diesels (total 1,300 bhp); 2 propellers.
Sensors: 1 of various sea search and navigational radars.
Armament: 1 single 20 mm Oerlikon anti-aircraft gun; 2 single
12.7 mm machine guns (no armament fitted to South African and UK
craft).
Top speed: 29 knots (Yemen); 27 knots (South African); 24 knots
(Sierra Leone and UK craft).　　**Range:** 650 nautical miles at 20 knots.
Programme: 8 of these craft have been sold to 4 naval users by
mid-1983 comprising South Africa's *P1554* and *P1555*, delivered in
1973; Yemen's craft, delivered in 1978; Sierra Leone's unit, delivered
in 1982, plus the Royal Navy's HMS *Attacker* (P281), HMS *Chaser*
(P282), HMS *Fencer* (P283), HMS *Hunter* (P284) and HMS *Striker*
(P285), all delivered in 1983.
Notes: Compact and seaworthy craft, all but the South African boats
are built throughout from glass-reinforced plastic.

Watercraft P2000 class   Patrol vessels

HMS Archer *(P264), lead of this Royal Navy fourteen craft class.*

Role: Coastal patrol and training.   **Builder:** Watercraft, UK.
Users: Navies of UK (14), Nigeria (2) and Omani Police (1).
Basic data: 43 (UK) to 49 (Oman) tons full displacement; 68.2 ft (20.8 m) on UK and Omani craft or 68.9 ft (21.0 m) for Nigerian's overall length; 19.0 ft (5.8 m) maximum beam.   **Crew:** Up to 11.
Propulsion: 2 diesels; 2 propellers comprising Rolls-Royce CV12 M800T (total 1,600 bhp) for UK or MTU 8V-396 (total 2,036 bhp) for Nigeria and MTU 12V-396 TB 93 (total 3,000 bhp) for Omani craft.
Sensors: 1 Racal-Decca AC1216C sea search and navigational radar.
Armament: None fitted as standard.
Top speed: 40 (Oman), over 30 (Nigeria), 22 (UK) knots.
Range: Over 700 (Oman) or 500 (UK and Nigeria) nautical miles at 18 (Oman), or 17 (Nigeria) or 15 (UK) knots.
Programme: The first craft, Oman's *Dheeb al Bahar I*, ordered in December 1983, was delivered in late 1984. In May 1984 the Royal Navy placed a contract for 14 of this class comprising: HMS *Archer* (P264), HMS *Biter* (P270), HMS *Smiter* (P272), HMS *Pursuer* (P273), HMS *Blazer* (P279), HMS *Dasher* (P280), HMS *Puncher* (P291), HMS *Charger* (P292), HMS *Ranger* (P293) and HMS *Trumpeter* (P294) for Royal Navy Reserve training service, along with *Loyal Example* (P153), *Loyal Explorer* (P154), *Loyal Express* (P163) and *Loyal Exploit* (P167) for Royal Navy Auxiliary Service use. Deliveries of the Royal Navy craft occur from August 1985 through to mid-1986. Nigeria ordered 2 slightly stretched, aluminium-hulled version in January 1985 for delivery in March 1986.
Notes: All P2000 craft employ a glass reinforced plastic construction, other than Nigeria's light alloy pair.

Wasp class

Assault ships

An artist's impression of USS Wasp *(LHD1) as completed.*

Role: Amphibious warfare. **Builder:** Ingalls Shipbuilding, USA.
User: US Navy.
Basic data: 40,500 tons full displacement; 840.0 ft (256.0 m) overall
length; 106.0 ft (32.3 m) maximum beam. **Crew:** 1,080.
Propulsion: 2 Westinghouse geared steam turbines (total
70,000 shp); 2 propellers.
Sensors: 1 SPS-52B long-range air search and height finder (3-D)
radar; SPS-49 long-range air search radar; 1 SPS-67 sea search and
navigational radar; 1 Mk 86 and 2 Mk 115 fire control radars; TACAN
aircraft homer; NTDS automated action information data processing
system.
Armament: Up to 43 helicopters; 2 Mk 25 octuple Sea Sparrow point
air defence missile launchers; 2 single 4.5-inch Mk 45 dual-purpose
guns; 3 Mk 15 Phalanx 20 mm close-in weapons systems.
Top speed: 24 knots. **Range:** 10,000 nautical miles at 20 knots.
Programme: Authorised in late 1981, the contract to proceed with
construction of the lead, USS *Wasp* (LHD1), of this 5 or more ship
class being placed at the end of 1983. *Wasp* should be in service by
the close of 1986.
Notes: While basically similar in both external appearance and internal
layout to the earlier Tarawa class, the Wasp class design will vary
considerably from its forebears in detail.

Brooke Marine 93 m class   Assault ships

Oman's Nasr Al Bahr (*L2*).

Role: Amphibious warfare.   **Builder:** Brooke Marine, UK.
Users: Algeria (2) and Oman (1).
Basic data: 2,200 tons full displacement; 305.1 ft (93.0 m) overall
length; 50.85 ft (15.5 m) maximum beam.   **Crew:** 81.
Propulsion: 2 MTU diesels (total 8,000 bhp); 2 propellers.
Sensors: 1 Decca TM1226 sea search and navigational radar; 1 fire
control radar and optronic fire director (customer choice); 1 Kelvin
Hughes MS45 echo sounder.
Armament: 2 single 40 mm Breda/Bofors L40/70 anti-aircraft guns.
Top speed: 16 knots.   **Range:** 3,000 nautical miles at 14 knots.
Programme: The initial order, for 2 ships, from Algeria was placed in
June 1981, the vessels, *Klaat Benni Hammid* and *Klaat Benni Rached*
(the construction of the latter ship being sub-contracted to Vosper
Thorneycroft), delivered in December 1983 and August 1984. Oman
ordered a single ship, *Nasr Al Bahr*, in May 1982, it being delivered in
early 1985.
Notes: This design is capable of transporting 380 tons of cargo right
up to the beach. Beyond the normal crew complement, each ship can
accommodate up to 240 troops and 7 heavyweight main battle tanks
plus a number of light and medium sized landing craft.

The French Navy's Francis Champlain (*L9030*).

Role: Amphibious warfare.   **Builders:** Various, France.
Users: Navies of France (6) and Morocco (3).
Basic data: 1,330 tons full displacement; 262.5 ft (80.0 m) overall length; 42.65 ft (13.0 m) maximum beam.   **Crew:** 39.
Propulsion: 2 SACM V12 diesels (total 1,800 bhp); 2 controllable-pitch propellers.
Sensors: 1 Decca TM1226 sea search and navigational radar; 1 echo sounder.
Armament: 2 single 40 mm anti-aircraft guns; 2 single 81 mm mortars; 2 single 12.7 mm machine guns. *Note:* an aft helipad is installed.
Top speed: 16 knots.   **Range:** 4,500 nautical miles at 13 knots.
Programme: 9 vessels of this class were known to have been ordered by mid-1983 comprising: *Champlain* (L9030), *Francis Garnier* (L9031), *Dumont D'Urville* (L9032), *Jacques Cartier* (L9033), plus *L9034* and *L9035* for France, along with *Daoud Ben Aicha* (LST42), *Ahmed Es Sakali* (LST 43) and *Abou Abdallah EL Ayachi* (LST44) for Morocco. The first 2 French vessels entered service in October and June 1974, respectively, followed by the second pair during 1983, at which time the 5th and 6th ships were fitting out. The 3 Moroccan vessels entered service in May 1977, September 1977 and December 1978, respectively.
Notes: The Champlain class have no vehicular drive-through capability, everything having to be embarked and disembarked through the bow ramp.

Abdiel type   Minelayers

The Royal Navy's HMS Abdiel *(N21) doubles as a minelayer and minehunter support tender.*

Role: Minelayer/tender.   **Builder:** J.I. Thornycroft, UK.
User: Royal Navy.
Basic data: 1,400 tons full displacement; 265.0 ft (80.8 m) overall length; 38.5 ft (11.7 m) maximum beam.   **Crew:** 96.
Propulsion: 2 Paxman Ventura 16-YSCM diesels (total 2,690 bhp); 2 propellers.
Sensors: 1 Type 978 sea search and navigational radar; 1 Decca Hi-Fix precision position fixer; 1 Kelvin Hughes MS45 echo sounder.
Armament: 1 single 40 mm Mk 9 Bofors L40/60 anti-aircraft gun; up to 44 mines.
Top speed: 16 knots.   **Range:** 3,200 nautical miles at 12 knots.
Programme: HMS *Abdiel* (N21), the Royal Navy's sole minelayer, started life as the second of a projected pair of mercantile car ferries planned to operate out of Malta. Laid down in May 1966 and launched in January 1967, HMS *Abdiel* entered service with the Royal Navy in October 1967.
Notes: Although employing none of the automated mine magazine-to-rail and dispensing systems to be found aboard the modern Scandinavian minelayers, HMS *Abdiel* still provides a useful training platform. Of equal importance operationally is *Abdiel's* extensive capability to act as mother ship to a mine countermeasures squadron.

Pohjanmaa type

Minelayers

Finland's Pohjanmaa (*N01*).

Role: Minelayer/training ship.
User: Finnish Defence Force.
Builder: Wartsila, Finland.
Basic data: 1,350 tons full displacement; 256.6 ft (78.2 m) overall length; 38.0 ft (11.6 m) maximum beam.
Crew: 80.
Propulsion: 2 Wartsila-Vasa 16V22 diesels (total 5,800 bhp); 2 controllable-pitch propellers.
Sensors: 1 air search radar; 1 sea search and navigational radar; 1 Philips (Sweden) 9 LV100 fire control radar and automated action information processing system; 2 hull-mounted sonars.
Armament: 1 single 120 mm Bofors TAK-120 dual-purpose gun; 2 single 40 mm Bofors anti-aircraft guns; 4 twin 23 mm anti-aircraft guns; 2 five-barrelled 250 mm RBU-1200 anti-submarine rocket launchers.
Top speed: 20 knots.   **Range:** 3,000 nautical miles at 17 knots.
Programme: *Pohjanmaa* (N01) was laid down in May 1978, launched in late August 1978 and entered service less than a year later in early 1979.
Notes: Constructed in a very short time at Wartsila's Helsinki yards, the *Pohjanmaa*'s design much more closely resembles that of a front line corvette than that of a typical minelayer.

Waveney class   Minehunters

HMS Waveney *(M2003), lead of class.*

Role: Ocean minesweeping.
Builder: Richards Shipbuilders, UK.   **User:** Royal Navy Reserve.
Basic data: 900 tons full displacement; 154.2 ft (47.0 m) overall
length; 34.4 ft (10.5 m) maximum beam.   **Crew:** 30.
Propulsion: 2 Ruston RKC diesels (total 3,040 bhp); 2 controllable-
pitch propellers.
Sensors: 2 Racal-Decca Type 1226 sea search and navigational ra-
dars; 2 Kelvin Hughes MS48 echo sounders.
Armament: 1 single 40 mm Bofors L40/60 anti-aircraft gun.
Top speed: 15.5 knots.   **Range:** Over 2,000 nautical miles.
Programme: A 12 ship class ordered on an incremental basis. The
lead of class, HMS *Waveney* (M2003), was ordered in September
1982, and was delivered in the spring of 1984. The rest of class com-
prise HMS *Carron* (M2004), HMS *Dovey* (M2005), HMS *Helford*
(M2006), HMS *Humber* (M2007), HMS *Blackwater* (M2008), HMS
Itchen (M2009), HMS *Helmsdale* (M2010), HMS *Orwell* (M2011),
HMS *Ribble* (M2012), HMS *Spey* (M2013) and HMS *Arun* (M2014).
The first 4 were in service by the end of April 1985, with the remaining
ships scheduled for delivery by 1987.
Notes: The Waveney class design is based on that of a commercial
North Sea supply boat. Built to mercantile Lloyds Register standards,
but with additional below-waterline compartments to minimise the
effects of nearby detonations, the fully equipped unit cost of the first
4 ship batch was around £4.75 million in late 1982 values.

Hatsushima class   Minehunters

Hatsushima (*MSC649*), *the lead ship of this new Japanese coastal minesweeping class.*

Role: Coastal minesweeper.
Builders: Nippon Kokan and Hitachi, Japan.
User: Japanese Maritime Self-Defence Force.
Basic data: 440 tons full displacement; 180.4 ft (55.0 m) overall length; 30.8 ft (9.4 m) maximum beam.   **Crew:** 45.
Propulsion: 2 Mitsubishi YV12ZC-15/20 diesels (total 1,440 bhp); 2 controllable-pitch propellers.
Sensors: 1 OPS 9 sea search and navigational radar; 1 ZQS 2B hull-mounted sonar.
Armament: 1 single 20 mm anti-aircraft gun or 20 mm Phalanx on later ships.
Top speed: 14 knots.   **Range:** Over 2,600 nautical miles at 8 knots.
Programme: A planned 19 ship class of which 17 had been started by mid-1985. The known ships comprise: *Hatsushima* (MSC649), *Ninoshima* (650), *Miyajima* (651), *Nenoshima* (652), *Ukishima* (653), *Ooshima* (654), *Niijima* (655), *Yukushima* (656), *Narushima* (657), along with the as yet unnamed 658 through 661. The lead of class was built by Nippon Kokan, and entered service at the end of March 1979. All should be delivered prior to the end of 1991.
Notes: These wooden construction vessels can operate in company as conventional minesweepers or singly as minehunters when deploying their Japanese-developed Type 54 mine neutralisation vehicle.

Cardinal class

Minehunters

An impression of USS Cardinal *(MSH 1) to be delivered in 1987.*

Role: Coastal minesweeping and minehunting.
Builder: Bell Aerospace Halter, USA. **User:** US Navy.
Basic data: 434 tons full displacement; 189.0 ft (57.6 m) overall length: 39.0 ft (11.9 m) maximum beam. **Crew:** 43 to 51.
Propulsion: 4 Waukesha L1616 DSIN diesels (total 2,400 bhp) with 2 used to drive 2 lift fans and 2 used to drive 2 propellers, plus providing craft's electrical and electro-hydraulic power.
Sensors: 1 SPS-64 sea search and navigational radar; 1 LN-66 sea search and navigational radar; SQQ-32 variable-depth sonar; 1 Honeywell mine neutralization vehicle.
Armament: None fitted.
Top speed: 25 knots. **Range:** 1,200 nautical miles at 12 knots.
Programme: The lead of this planned 17 vessel class, USS *Cardinal* (MSH 1) was ordered in November 1984 for a scheduled entry into service during 1987. A 2nd of class is planned for 1989 delivery, followed by accelerating deliveries continuing well into the 1990s.
Notes: Employing the British-developed rigid side-wall, air-cushion principle taken up by Bell Halter, the Cardinal class will be constructed primarily of glass reinforced plastic/foam sandwich as developed by Karlskronavaret in Sweden. The Cardinal class are primarily destined to be homeported at strategic bases around the US continental coastline from which it is assumed that they would be operating within friendly airspace, hence the lack of need for anti-air defences.

Boris Chilikin class
Replenishers

The Soviet Navy's Boris Chilikin *fleet replenisher.*

Role: Underway replenishment.
Builder: Baltic Shipyard, USSR.   **User:** Soviet Navy.
Basic data: 24,500 tons full displacement; 532.5 ft (162.3 m) overall
length: 70.2 ft (21.4 m) maximum beam.   **Crew:** 320.
Propulsion: 1 unidentified diesel (9,600 bhp); 1 propeller.
Sensors: 1 sea search and navigational radar; provision to fit 1 fire
control radar for guns; satellite-fed data link and precision position
fixing.
Armament: Provision to mount 2 twin 57 mm anti-aircraft guns on
forward section plinths.
Top speed: 17 knots.   **Range:** 10,000 nautical miles at 16 knots.
Programme: This 6-ship class, built between 1971 and 1978, comprises: *Boris Chilikin, Dnestr, Genric Gasanov, Ivan Bubnov, Boris
Butoma* and *Vladimir Kolyachitskiy.*
Notes: Based on the Soviet mercantile Velikiy Oktyabr class tanker
design, each Chilikins class is capable of carrying approximately
15,100 tons of bulk liquids, including around 1,600 tons of diesel oil
for the ship's own use, plus another 1,200 tons of ammunition, dry provisions and equipment spares. The number and position of the liquid
transfer stations varies from one ship to another, ranging from two to
five, as can readily be discerned from a photographic analysis of the
class.

Deepak class

Replenishers

Shakti (*A57*), *the second of a two ship Indian Navy class*.

Role: Underway replenishment.
Builder: Bremer Vulkan, Federal Germany.   **User:** Indian Navy.
Basic data: 22,000 tons full displacement; 552.6 ft (168.4 m) overall
length; 75.5 ft (23.0 m) maximum beam.   **Crew:** 169.
Propulsion: 1 geared steam turbine (16,500 shp); 1 propeller.
Sensors: 1 Decca sea search and navigational radar.
Armament: 3 single 40 mm Bofors and 2 single 20 mm Oerlikon
anti-aircraft guns. Helipad and hangar for Sea King (not normally car-
ried).
Top speed: 20 knots.   **Range:** 5,500 nautical miles at 18.5 knots.
Programme: This 2 ship Indian Navy class comprises: *Deepak* (A50)
and *Shakti* (A57); the service entry dates for which were November
1972 and February 1976, respectively.
Notes: These ships can each carry up to 15,800 tons of cargo, of
which 12,624 tons is fuel oil, 1,280 tons of diesel fuel and 1,495 tons
of aviation kerosene, leaving 401 tons for solid stores and provisions.
The Deepak class is fitted with two liquid transfer stations per side,
enabling it to replenish two accompanying ships simultaneously.

Challenger type

Support ships

HMS Challenger (*K07*).

Role: Seabed rescue and salvage.
Builder: Scott Lithgow, UK.   **User:** Royal Navy.
Basic data: 7,573 tons full displacement; 439.6 ft (184 m) overall length; 59.1 ft (18 m) maximum beam.   **Crew:** 173.
Propulsion: 5 Ruston 16RK3ACZ diesel electric generator (total 17,150 bhp); 1 cycloid propeller, plus 3 bow thrusters.
Sensors: 1 Kelvin Hughes Type 1006 navigational radar; 1 Marconi/Decca Hydroplot; 1 Type 162M and 193M hull-mounted sonars, plus 1 Type 2003 and 2013 towed array sonars.
Armament: Nil, but facilities to operate up to Sea King-sized helicopters.
Top speed: 15 knots.   **Range:** 8,000 nautical miles at 15 knots.
Programme: Ordered in September 1979, HMS *Challenger* (K07) was launched in May 1981 and commissioned in August 1984.
Notes: The ship is equipped with a large, 2-element, unmanned tethered submersible system, capable of reconnoitring the seabed down to depths of around 950 feet (300 m) and out to ranges of over 26,000 feet (7,925 m). In the case of rescue from a sunken submarine, the ship carries a large, 3-man operated diving bell, that can hold up to 12 survivors in its twin chambers. To handle heavy duty salvage work, the ship carries a 25-ton-lift crane just forward of its side-by-side funnels.

KNM Horten (*A530*).

Role: Transport/tender.   **Builder:** Horten Shipyard, Norway.
User: Royal Norwegian Navy.
Basic data: 2,500 tons full displacement; 285.4 ft (87.0 m) overall
length; 44.9 ft (13.7 m) maximum beam.   **Crew:** 86.
Propulsion: 2 Wichman 7AX diesels (total 4,200 bhp); 2 propellers;
1 bow thruster.
Sensors: 2 Decca 1226 sea search and navigational radars.
Armament: 1 Westland Lynx helicopter; 2 single 40 mm Bofors anti-
aircraft guns.
Top speed: 16.5 knots.
Range: Over 3,500 nautical miles at 12 knots.
Programme: Ordered at the end of March 1976, KNM *Horten* (A530)
was laid down in late January 1977, launched in August 1977 and
entered service in early June 1978.
Notes: Typical of the modern multi-purpose naval design, KNM *Horten* has a rather stark, tall, rectangular superstructure, topped by squat,
staggered, side-mounted funnels. Although primarily designed as a
support tender for the Royal Norwegian Navy's numerous submarines
and fast attack craft, *Horten* can double as a troop and equipment
transport, having accommodation for a further 190 personnel in addition to the normal ship's complement.

INDEX OF WARSHIP CLASSES AND TYPES